Michon carefully pulled the canoe partway onto the rocky shore, then stood before Chas, her clothes soaking wet and clinging to every inch of her form. She was chilled, but the look she saw on Chas's face sent warmth coursing through her body.

"Do you have any idea how beautiful you are?" His voice was husky.

She shook her head. "Please, don't tease me. I must look like a drowned rat."

"No, you don't," he whispered. "You look natural, the way I want a woman to look." Chas reached out and took her into his arms, wrapping her tightly in his embrace.

Michon was pressed against his chest, helpless and totally willing to stay where she was. She felt secure in his arms in a way she hadn't believed possible.

But this was more than security....

River
Rapture

VELLA MUNN

Harlequin Books

TORONTO • NEW YORK • LONDON
AMSTERDAM • PARIS • SYDNEY • HAMBURG
STOCKHOLM • ATHENS • TOKYO • MILAN

Chapter One

Michon Lycan slipped out of the bucket seat of her two-year-old compact car, locked the door, and paused to adjust the leather belt on her lavender jumpsuit. Even with her discount at Chantilla the outfit had cost a week's salary. This was the first day she had worn it; shouldn't she be facing the next eight hours with enthusiasm?

But for some reason Michon could put no name to, which had been growing ever stronger for the past month, her feet in their white high-heeled sandals were dragging. Being in charge of the sportswear department for Chantilla was supposed to be one of the most glamorous jobs a woman in the southern part of Oregon could hope for. Hadn't Michon given up the mind-draining secretarial job she'd held for two years to take advantage of a rare opening in the most exclusive dress shop in the city? Her friends could barely contain their envy when Michon told them. "Have you seen the women who work there? What exquisite creatures! They're always being called to model at fashion shows. And the customers! You can bet they don't worry about paying the gas bill."

been going to college and burning the candle at both ends.

Michon was experimenting with some jewelry changes on a pair of mannequins wearing lace body suits in complementary pastels when Traci Black from lingerie wandered by. "How much are those little numbers?" Traci asked, nodding approval as Michon slipped a thin gold chain around a mannequin's neck.

Michon grimaced. "Don't ask. How these outfits wound up in sportswear instead of lingerie is beyond me. Can you imagine anyone doing exercises in fabric that delicate?"

Traci winked. "There's exercise, and then there's exercise. Besides, who are we trying to kid? The women who come into Chantilla aren't looking for sweat shirts to pull on while they jog around the block. They have to look chic at the health club. Status. That's what we sell."

"At this price they'll get all the status their pocketbooks can stand. I sure as heck wouldn't waste money on that worthless fabric—if I had the money to throw away. What are you doing here?" Michon asked. "I thought you were waiting on Mr. Wilkins."

It was Traci's turn to grimace. "The distinguished attorney purchased the required garment necessary to take care of his responsibilities for his wife's birthday. He also picked up a satin nightgown with a slit that comes clear up to the hipbones. Something makes me think that little number isn't for Mrs. Wilkins."

"Traci!" Michon gasped in mock horror. "You have a suspicious mind."

"Just being honest. All I can say is Jim better not ever buy nightgowns for anyone but me." Traci dropped her

Traci's words stayed with her, even after a trio of matrons came into the store and Michon busied herself waiting on them. What Traci had said was striking a cord deep inside her, one she was beginning to admit she'd been trying to ignore for too long. As she discussed the relative merits of a hooded jacket versus a velour jogging outfit with a woman who was much more interested in style than practicality, Michon let her eyes roam over Chantilla's ample floor space. Modernistic mannequins on raised platforms served to distinguish the different departments. Elevator music and the inescapable scent of filtered air, plus the deep sound-cushioning carpeting, gave Michon the feeling that the owners were determined to keep out anything that might detract from a total aura of elegance. A small measure of sunlight was allowed in through tinted windows, but the windows were obviously second in importance to the rich fabric wall covering on the high walls, the recessed ceiling lights. Price tags were small and discreetly placed. There were no garish sale signs, no bargain tables. But what struck Michon most was that except for the staff's ability to move about, the saleswomen and mannequins appeared to be interchangeable.

Did her own face register as little emotion as she was seeing on the faces of other employees? Was that because they were all afraid of disturbing their carefully applied makeup, or because being within Chantilla's walls reduced people to be stereotypes of the Chantilla image? Cool and aloof described the employees all right. The question Michon didn't like facing was whether emotions could continue to exist in such a sterile exterior location.

cated for herself lately by asking questions about where she was heading in her life. Why did she insist on trying to find out why she no longer woke up eager to go to work, whether she really wanted to put so much of her salary on her back.

"Maybe I just need a vacation," she told the squirrel. "That's it. Everyone needs a break, a change of pace." She opened her second diet bar, stared at it, and then impulsively broke off a piece for the squirrel. "How about a little bribe?" she asked the rodent, who'd moved back a few steps while he lunched on a combination of nuts, coconut, and preservatives held together with honey. "You go to work for me this afternoon. You smile nice for the customers. I'll stay here and keep my eye out for handouts."

"That sounds like an even trade."

Michon started, found the source of the deep masculine voice, and stared up at the man standing over her. The sun was behind him so she had to squint, which reduced his features to a blurred, vague outline. "I—" she started and then tried again. "This was a private conversation."

"Kind of one-sided, wouldn't you say?" the shadowy figure clad in dark clothes asked. "I've yet to meet a squirrel who was much of a conversationalist."

Michon scrambled to her feet, hoping the tall stranger wouldn't guess she was doing so because she wanted to lessen the feeling that she was being dominated by his size. "Maybe not, but he's a good listener," she said. "How much of this did you eavesdrop on?"

"Not much. Can anyone really get fat on that junk you fed him?"

Not much! That was a likely story. He'd probably

too. "Do you put, you know, stuff on your hair?" he asked.

Michon looked up at him. Now she could make out his features—thick black eyebrows, deep-set eyes, slightly sunburned nose, a little-boy quality to the smile that revealed perfect teeth, except for a small chip on one of the lower ones. "What are you talking about?" Should she be offended? It was hard to know, because she was more interested in deciding whether blue or black dominated in his eyes.

"Well, I don't really know." His boyish, almost shy, grin started up again. "I mean your hair is kind of blond, but it's almost white in places. Does hair really come that way?"

Michon laughed, her first honest laugh of the day. "With a little help. That's called streaking. Do you always ask such personal questions of women you've just met?"

He shrugged. "I was curious. By the way, do you know where I might be able to pick up a Duluth pack around here?"

"A what? I've never heard of that."

"Never mind. Is this where you work?" the man indicated the ornate brass handles leading the way into Chantilla. "I've never been inside a place like that."

"Why not?" Michon wasn't just talking to keep the conversation going. She really wanted to know. A man wearing a chambray shirt with an unironed collar turning up at the ends would turn a head or two in Chantilla, especially when he filled out his faded jeans the way this man did. Somehow she couldn't imagine him ever being comfortable in one of the raw silk jackets displayed on the male mannequins.

"I don't want to make you late. It was nice talking to you." Before she knew it was going to happen, he'd spun lightly and was walking away from her.

Michon stared after him, noting the athletic grace to his walk, the hard line of his legs, the powerful shoulders straining against the well-worn shirt. What was his name? She hadn't learned that simple fact, and yet he'd affected her in a way that reminded her of what it felt like to be singled out by the football captain during the high school prom.

It wasn't fair! He shouldn't be allowed to drift in and out of her life so casually. But what could she do? She could hardly imagine herself running after him, telling him they couldn't let things end like this. She might be modern and liberated, but that didn't mean she could tell a stranger that the rest of her day was going to feel hollow because he'd left.

Michon was barely aware of what she was doing as she went inside and pasted on a smile before waiting on a customer. She ran through the standard nonsense about understanding that the customer wanted to make a fashion statement and that it was her job to help make that statement the most effective, but as she steered the woman to a line of crushed-velvet pants, her mind was on faded blue jeans, worn shoes, and a man who couldn't care less whether he ever set foot in Chantilla.

It wasn't until later in the afternoon that Michon found herself without a customer to muddy up her thoughts. Why had she let him go so easily? And yet he didn't strike her as the kind of man who would understand a woman who batted her lashes and made veiled hints about getting to know each other better. Maybe she didn't know his name, but instinct told her that he

"I don't like working here."

Traci clapped a hand over Michon's mouth. "Don't say that! The walls have ears. Come on, kid. Where else could we command the salaries we do and be nothing more than saleswomen? All that money and status and darn little responsibility. We have it made here."

"Do we?" Michon turned anguished eyes on her friend. "You know what I was thinking this morning? I was looking at the mannequins and thinking that that's all we really are. Walking, talking mannequins. Put a voice box in those figurines, and they could do our jobs."

"You're getting weird. You know that, don't you?" Traci asked. "I'm not too crazy about the forty-hour week myself, but then my mind is on a certain man and what I'd rather be doing. What's your excuse?"

"I just met a man."

"Just? What about Paul? Forget Paul. What's this man's name?"

"I don't know," Michon groaned. "Traci, I don't know!"

It would be romantic to think that it was the stranger who was doing these things to her emotions. But Michon admitted that he was simply the catalyst that was making her finally face her dissatisfaction with her life. Her life had been clean and neat and orderly and in keeping with images formed by fashion magazines. He was like a cowboy thundering into a sleepy frontier town to shake its foundations. But the foundations weren't as strong as she'd tried to make them, or they wouldn't be so badly shaken.

You've been working too hard, old girl. You need a vacation, she told herself as she wrestled with deciding between going home and dropping in at the deli near the supermarket.

That was it. She hadn't had more than two days off since she went to work at Chantilla. Where would she go if she could get a week or more off? There was always her parents, but seeing them would be like stepping back in time, when what she really needed was territory she'd never explored before. Her grandfather would have understood. He'd always listened to everything she said. But he was dead now and Michon was on her own.

Michon dropped her keys back in her purse and took off for the deli. So what if she went off her diet? A woman couldn't live forever on lettuce and diet bars, could she? Besides, she wanted to sit down and think about this vacation business, not have to worry about throwing a meal together. Swiss cheese, ham, rye bread. That's what she needed to get her thoughts organized.

She walked into the deli, made a mental note of the crisp gingham tablecloths over rustic tables, and stood

"Hi. Sit down. That looks better than whatever you were eating for lunch."

"You're right about that," Michon acknowledged as she positioned her legs under the tiny table. Their legs brushed. "This is no way to stay on a diet, but it sure smells good."

"Why are you on a diet?" he asked as he bit into his own meal. "You're skinny."

Skinny? It wasn't exactly a compliment. "The whole world's on a diet," she laughed. "I wouldn't want to think I wasn't playing the game. Besides, if I ate the way I wanted to I'd have to buy a whole new wardrobe."

"You wouldn't if you exercised enough." The way he was staring at her gave her the uneasy feeling that he was measuring the amount of muscle on her frame. "Exercise burns up the calories."

"I know." She sighed. "I've tried running, but by the time I get off work, the streets don't look very inviting or safe. And those health clubs are so expensive. So I diet." Michon wrinkled up her nose. "Let's not talk about diets. What are you doing here?"

"Shopping, or trying to." He stretched out in his chair and momentarily closed his eyes. "I'm going to lose my mind if I have to do much more of that. I hate shopping in the city. At least I got most of the gear I'll need. I've never taken a bunch of teenagers before. It's a whole new ball game."

"Wait a minute. What are you talking about? No"— Michon held up her hand as he started to open his mouth—"first things first. My name is Michon Lycan. What's yours?"

"Chas. Chas Carson of Carson River Tours. I don't

"How do any of us get started doing what we do?" He gave her a wry smile. "Do you really want to hear the whole story?"

"Of course."

"Okay, I just hope it won't bore you." He stopped for a minute, as if organizing his thoughts. "I was always more interested in planning some adventure than in going to school. I took to scouting like a puppy takes to an old slipper. I joined the sheriff department's search-and-rescue team where I was going to college. That really turned me on. I attended several workshops on wilderness survival, became a paramedic, did mountain climbing. The whole macho bit. But it wasn't until I went canoeing as part of a wilderness expedition that I decided what I wanted to do with my life. I've been accused of acting like a little boy following in the footsteps of Kit Carson or Daniel Boone. I may never get rich, but at least I won't wind up getting killed in some freeway accident." He laughed. "I'll probably wind up smashing myself against a submerged boulder."

Michon knew he was joking, but the thought of Chas Carson being dashed against a boulder in a foaming, angry river miles from any hospital sent a shudder through her. If she had her way, she'd wrap him in a terry cloth robe and hold him tightly against her.

What was she thinking! Michon dipped her head, hoping her makeup hid the flames she felt on her cheeks. Chas Carson was hardly the kind of man who would allow a woman to dictate what he did with his life. Some instinct she didn't argue with told her that. To stop her thoughts, Michon concentrated on getting Chas to tell her more about his unique way of life. "I'm

talk, now that physical contact had been made between them, but she felt it important to make the effort. "It's been on my mind a lot these days. I need a vacation or something."

"Or something?" Chas's eyes narrowed until they were mere slits, but that didn't stop the dark light from showing through. "There's no end to the possibilities in a statement like that." His voice was even deeper than usual as he spoke.

Michon started. Did he think she was referring to something sexual in nature? She'd been feeling unbelievably relaxed talking to a man she barely knew, but maybe he was getting an entirely different message. Did he think she was trying to tell him that she was available, willing? "I'm afraid you misunderstood me," she said icily, drawing her hand away. "I happen to have a boyfriend."

Chas blinked. "I'm glad you have a boyfriend, but what does that have to do with what we're talking about?"

"I mean"—she stood up and started to turn away— "I don't believe in one-night stands."

Chas stopped her before she could reach the door. He grabbed her arm firmly and yet gently and steered her outside where their fellow diners couldn't hear. She thought about struggling but his touch effectively filled her muscles with a sense of inertia. He easily pinned her against the deli's outer wall and forced her to meet his penetrating eyes. His voice was firm, almost rough. "I don't know what's got you all in a lather, but there's one thing I want you to understand. I don't have much use for one-night stands. If you misunderstood me, I'm sorry. I happen to enjoy talking to you. Can't we

Michon slipped into her seat and picked up her sandwich. "Do you really eat freeze-dried food?" she asked, feeling a little foolish about her behavior. Righteous indignation didn't really go with the situation. She hadn't meant to imply that she was making fun of his social skills. She wasn't comfortable with the thought that they were misunderstanding each other this much.

Chas gave her a thumbnail sketch of the type of food planning necessary for a week-long canoeing expedition for twenty teenagers. Michon tried to concentrate on what he was saying, but kept getting distracted. It was much more interesting to watch his habit of clenching his jaws at the end of a sentence, the expressive moves of his large calloused hands, the quick interplay of blue and black in his eyes. Michon allowed her eyes to glaze over slightly as she tried to picture him in a three-piece suit instead of his faded, unironed shirt. No. That was as unnatural as teaching wild animals to perform for a circus.

"When will you be leaving? Where are you going?" she asked, suddenly aware that the conversation revolved around the fact that soon he would be kneeling in a canoe instead of sitting across from her.

"In exactly eight days. The John Day River is about right for the skills of the kids I'll be leading."

"Have you ever done anything like that before? I mean, I know you're a guide, but teenagers are so full of energy. They don't always have their brains engaged. I don't know if I'd have the courage to take that on."

"They've all had some wilderness training," Chas explained. "It's not as if they've never been out on their own before. And their teacher is going along, so he'll be responsible for keeping them in line. He's try-

"In other words I'd survive if there was someone there to keep an eye on me, but I wouldn't be much help?" she asked, not sure she was ready for an honest answer.

"That's about the size of it," Chas answered, apparently unconcerned with whether he was being too blunt. "Look, Michon, you work in a dress shop, you wear expensive clothes. I'm willing to bet you don't drive an old pickup like me. I'm out of my element in the city; you'd be out of yours on a river."

Michon closed her eyes, thinking, despite herself, about spending the rest of her life waiting on matrons at Chantilla. "Don't you ever want a challenge, to test yourself?" she whispered, speaking more to herself than to Chas. "Or do you have everything you want?"

"I thought I did. Once."

Michon opened her eyes, but there was a veil over Chas's eyes. Only his words remained. Was he talking about having love and losing it? No! She wasn't going to think about that. "I—I'm sorry," she stammered. "I didn't mean to ask a personal question."

"And I didn't have to answer. Forget I said anything. Look, I hate to say this, but I really have a lot to do. I'm supposed to meet with the kids' teacher this evening. That's the other reason I'm in the city today."

"Oh." Chas's words were simple and straightforward, but they had the power to throw her into a nameless depression. He was leaving her already? "I—well, I enjoyed talking to you."

"So did I. Look, I know you have a boyfriend and all that, but I'd like to see you again some time. Just to talk, I mean."

"Do you like your car?" Chas asked as she was getting out her keys.

"It's okay. It gets me where I need to get."

"It looks like a toy." Chas shook his head. "I just can't imagine myself with one of those. I'd high-center it for sure the first time I took it on a dirt road."

"I don't get out on dirt roads that much," Michon pointed out, for some reason feeling as if she had to defend her choice of transportation.

After Michon had gotten in and rolled down the window, Chas leaned against the door. "We don't have a whole lot in common, you know."

"I don't agree," she protested. But what else could she say? She could hardly tell him that she couldn't ever remember wanting to spend more time with any man than she wanted to at this moment. "We both like deli sandwiches," she finished weakly.

"You're high fashion," he said softly. "I'm Daniel Boone."

"No I'm not," she protested. She ran shaking fingers through her tinted hair. "I look like this because it's required in my job. There's more to me than hair and painted fingernails."

Chas didn't speak. Instead his eyes bore into hers, past their scant defense and deep inside, where something nameless and warm and hungry was stirring. She knew what he was saying and lifted her face in willing response.

Their kiss spanned whatever differences existed.

so, but that didn't stop him from continuing to ask her to "help me out just this one last time." "I'm tired," she gave as excuse. "It's been a long day and Worthless needs a little attention."

"So do I, honey. Who means more to you—that mutt or me?"

Tired and confused as she was, Michon was in no mood to debate that with Paul. "I have to change my clothes."

"We'll be there in fifteen minutes. What about that new long dress of yours? The one with the slit. Knock his eyes out."

Paul hung up before she had time to respond. Michon returned the receiver to its cradle and held Worthless against her. " 'Knock his eyes out,' " she parroted sarcastically. "Show him a little flesh. Worthless, I don't think I'm going to like this." For a moment she rubbed noses with the delighted pup. "You've got it made, old boy. If I were smelly and ugly like you, no one would ever want to take me out. Come on. Keep me company while I try to find something to cover up my bones."

Worthless trotted after Michon and jumped up on the bed as she peered listlessly into her closet. She hadn't been lying. Her feet ached from wearing high heels all day, and there was nothing she'd like better than to sprawl in a chair. If she spent the evening in her apartment with no one except Worthless to talk to, she might have too much time to think . . . about a kiss and a man who didn't smell like expensive cologne. But she didn't want to think about something he'd said. He once thought he had everything he wanted. How deeply had that affected him and the relationships he formed?

grabbed at a long white skirt and a pale blue blouse with a high lace collar. Once dressed she had to admit she looked like a rather feminine takeoff of a frontier woman. She slipped into flat sandals and wiggled her toes in delight because they weren't hampered by hose. "I think I like you better like this," she told her image in the bedroom mirror. "I wonder if Chas Carson would approve?"

Hearing Chas's name spoken aloud instantly changed Michon's mood. She sank onto the bed, unmindful of any wrinkles that might form in her skirt. She lay back flattening her hair on the pillow, rubbing Worthless's head absently. She was too young for a midlife crisis...so what was the matter with her? First she was getting sick to her stomach just thinking about spending another year making polite conversation with Chantilla's wealthy customers. Then she'd started talking to squirrels. And now she was remembering how the world stood still when Chas Carson kissed her.

He was right. They were different. Totally different. She honestly didn't know there were men like him left in the twentieth century. A river guide? Did men really still do that kind of thing?

They must. Obviously that was how Chas made his living. He was a man's man in the old-fashioned tradition. He was experienced in search-and-rescue, lived the majority of his life out-of-doors, and by his own admission felt like a bull in a china shop in the city. Michon, for her part, had grown up on the city's limits in a standard tract home paid for by working parents. She'd gone to college because that's what all her friends were doing, had gone after the job considered "in" at the time, had found herself a modern apart-

"Beats the heck out of me," Michon said over her shoulder as she stepped out the door, plainly indicating that Paul should join her. "Besides, I believe the word is *ask*, not *tell*."

"You're in a fine mood," Paul said as he locked the door behind them. "Look, this guy is important."

"I know," Michon sighed. "Give me a little credit. I'm sorry," she relented. "I told you I was tired."

"I don't know why," Paul said. "You're the one who's always saying you've got a cushy job. Nothing to do but keep your lipstick in place and smile nicely at the ladies with the fat pocketbooks."

"Those are your words, not mine," Michon reminded him. "Don't you ever get tired of staring at the same four walls and saying the same things every day? That's what I'm tired of."

"Not as long as it pays the bills and paves the way to a promotion," Paul pointed out as they walked to where his car was parked. "You just need more challenges in your job. Anything can get stale if it stays the same long enough."

"You hit the nail on the head about that one," she agreed, accepting his hand on her arm as he helped her into the car. In the backseat sat a stocky, balding man cinched into a three-piece suit. For a moment Michon thought she wasn't going to win her war with the giggles. Except for the color of their suits and the sizes, both Paul and the stranger could have come out of the same cookie cutter. She forced herself to smile pleasantly as Paul introduced her to Joseph McCullum. Paul said something about Mr. McCullum being involved in manufacturing in Chicago, but Michon barely listened.

Now that she thought about it, she realized she knew

about? Did he wonder what moved her to tears? Someone to share an evening with, to keep from being alone
wasn't a good enough reason for blending their lives,
was it?

Paul pulled up in front of one of his favorite night
spots and gave Joseph a glowing description of the vari-
ety of drinks the bartender could mix. Michon listened,
thinking that her usual order of white wine sounded
pretty dull alongside the concoctions they were describ-
ing. But then Michon wasn't much of a drinker. Thank
heavens that was one thing Paul finally understood. He
didn't say much when she nursed a slim glass until the
liquid turned to room temperature.

Usually when she'd been talked into coming along
on one of Paul's expeditions into the city's nightlife
with a client, Michon made an effort to enter the conversation. But tonight her mind simply wouldn't settle
on the words swirling around her. Instead she found
herself staring at the plush, darkened interior of the
Blue Moon Lounge. Mahogany had been used to panel
the walls and form the top of the bar. Rich blue drapes
hung in full folds from the high windows. The only
light came from candles placed on each table. The interior was carefully designed to take customers away
from the everyday world and give them a feeling of
relaxed luxury.

But the effect was lost on Michon. She felt closed in,
confined, with the drapes and paneled walls hiding the
night sky. While they were driving over she'd noticed
that the moon was half full. What was wrong with letting a little of the silent, timeless night in?

Michon remembered sleeping out under the stars at
summer camp when she was a girl. Her parents con-

Joseph asked a few polite questions about what she did for a living and then asked Paul if he'd mind if she danced with him. Naturally Paul didn't mind. Michon slowly got to her feet, resigned to a slow, shuffling waltz pressed against Joseph's thick belly. The trio playing on the small stage in one corner of the lounge seemed to be falling asleep on the job. Michon couldn't help but wonder if this was the way they wanted to be spending their evening.

That didn't seem to bother Joseph. As they danced he kept up a nonstop monologue about his business dealings, his new car, the money he had in investments. If he was trying to impress Michon she couldn't help but wonder why he bothered. There was something about the stiff way he held her that told her he wasn't used to dancing with many women. She could be wrong, but Michon was willing to bet there was a Mrs. McCullum back in Chicago. There were probably children as well—teenagers wanting cars, trying to decide what college they were going to ask their father to put them through.

It struck Michon as terribly sad. Joseph McCullum was miles away from his family, spending the evening with two people he barely knew. He might even be entertaining the idea that the young woman with him could be talked into going to his motel room—not that that would ever happen. Was that what he really wanted out of life? When he'd been a young man, was this what he thought his future would be?

Life takes some unkind twists, Michon thought. We start out with such high hopes, but, bit by bit, they're replaced by reality. Family responsibilities, the need to earn a living, a thousand unplanned turns in one's life,

else. Besides, I don't have any choices left. I have to make the best of what I have."

Michon allowed Joseph to start steering her back to the table, but his words didn't leave her. Just before they reached Paul she stopped. "If you had your life to do over, what would you change?" Maybe she had no right asking him such a personal question, but she felt she had to know... for her sake.

Joseph's smile was wistful, but he seemed to need to talk. "I'd like to take a few chances. I wouldn't settle for what was safe. And I'd look for a woman who understood what I was talking about."

By the time they joined Paul, Michon was fighting tears. She was sad for Joseph McCullum and the life he'd settled for. But she was also sad for what she was now very much afraid was going to happen to her if she didn't do something about the direction her life was taking.

Take chances, he'd said. Find someone who understands.

Michon looked at Paul, who was grinning like a cat who'd just swallowed a canary because he thought he was showing his client the time of his life. Was he happy with his life? Michon rather suspected that the answer was yes. The only problem was that what Paul wanted out of life wasn't what Michon wanted. As her hands strayed over the lines of her fragile wineglass she realized that having a cupboard full of cut-glass wineglasses was so far down on the list of things she wanted out of life that it didn't even fit on the page.

She had no idea what time it was when Paul finally said they should leave. Although her eyes burned from the cigarette smoke and her head ached from the non-

depends on how clients react to me. I just thought I could count on you to be sensitive to that."

"I am. But, Paul, it isn't my world. Maybe I shouldn't feel like this, but I don't want to spend my life catering to the whims of other people. Okay, so I'm selfish, but I want to do something for me."

Paul's look showed that he didn't know what she was talking about. "Like what? I swear, you're not making any sense at all tonight."

"I'm not?"

"Hell, no. What do you mean, do something for yourself? Do you want a new apartment, another car? A spring outfit? Is that what you're talking about?"

Material things. Was that the only kind of wanting Paul could relate to? Michon shook her head, feeling wrung out because she was becoming more and more convinced that she and Paul weren't speaking the same language. "No. That's not it at all," she tried. "Paul, I don't like my job. I don't like what's happening, or not happening, in my life. I feel like I'm on a treadmill, going nowhere."

"Do you want to get married?"

Michon stared openmouthed at Paul's profile in the car's dark interior. He couldn't have shocked her more if he'd asked her if she wanted to rob a bank. Marriage was a word that had never come up between them. "No," she whispered.

Paul sighed loudly. "That's a relief. Look, don't get me wrong. I don't blame you for wanting to get married—it's what women still want—but I'm not ready to settle down yet. I thought you understood that about me, but the way you're talking tonight, well, I wasn't sure."

knowledge that she had finally seen through the shallowness of their relationship. They'd gone together because she wanted someone in her life, even the wrong someone.

But no more. "Someone" wasn't enough. Joseph McCullum had said it. Take chances. Don't settle for what's safe. Paul was safe. And Michon was ready, eager, to step beyond that.

She was ready for the John Day River. If it—and Chas—would give her the chance.

Despite a couple of wrong turns, Michon finally located the door marked Physical Education Department. If Mr. Bishop hadn't already agreed to see her this afternoon, Michon might have lost courage and scurried back to her car.

But she'd come this far. She'd taken the afternoon off, gathered her mental arguments, even gone through a receptionist, the assistant principal, and a counselor to locate the man in charge of the John Day canoeing expedition. She'd said little about her reason for wanting to talk to Mr. Bishop, reasoning that her arguments would be better made in person.

The man who looked up from a small, cluttered desk flanked by nylon mesh bags filled with basketballs and a pile of unclaimed shirts, shorts, and socks wasn't much taller than Michon, but his broad shoulders, bull neck, and lettered sweat shirt clearly identified him as a member of the physical education department.

He stood up, kicked aside an equipment bag, and stuck out a massive hand. "Miss Lycan. Did you have any trouble finding this place? It can be an adventure for someone who doesn't know her way around the school."

"I'm here," Michon said as she returned the handshake. "And you're right. I don't know my way around this place. I went to school here a while ago, but there have been several additions since then. I'm afraid my memory isn't as good as I thought it was."

"You went to school here? You didn't happen to have Mr. Allison for English did you? He's been here about twenty years. Excuse me." Harold Bishop grinned. "I'm sure you're here for something other than traipsing

of it. Mentioning Chas's name might help her cause. If possible she didn't want to tell Mr. Bishop that her relationship with Chas was only of one day's duration. "Actually Chas mentioned that you might not have a woman able to accompany the girls. When I was in college I spent two summers as a camp counselor. I've had experience planning camp-outs, that sort of thing." Michon could only hope that Mr. Bishop wouldn't press her into having to admit that the summer camp-outs were a far cry from what was on her mind now.

"And you're interested in the John Day expedition? I'm sorry if I sound confused." Mr. Bishop stopped working with the hand grips and ran his fingers through his graying hair. "I'm afraid it wouldn't be a real job. There's no money in the school's budget to pay you."

"Oh no," Michon interrupted. "I have a job. Did you think I was applying for one?"

"That was my first impression." Mr. Bishop grinned. "I must admit I was flattered. Not too many people are beating down the doors asking to get in on my crazy little project. The truth was, I had to secure private funding for the expedition before the school board would give its okay. But, back to what you're saying. The students and Chas and I are going to be away from civilization for about a week. Are you sure you can commit yourself to that much time?"

She wasn't being turned down! At least not without being allowed to plead her case. Michon gripped her hands together in her lap, still not completely understanding why this meant so much to her. "I have the vacation time coming," she said briefly, not bothering to explain that she wasn't sure she'd return to Chantilla even after the expedition was over.

ise you, I'll finish what I start." She decided to open up completely. "I feel as if I'm going crazy at work these days. I need to get away, learn a little more about myself."

Mr. Bishop's puzzled look prompted Michon to continue. "I'm tired of playing it safe. I want to see what I'm really made of. I need that. When Chas started telling me about the expedition, something about it set off a spark inside me. It's what I need."

The line on Mr. Bishop's phone rang, breaking Michon's concentration. As he responded to the call Michon attempted to distract herself by looking around the room, but the conversation held her attention. Apparently Mr. Bishop was trying to convince the caller not to drop some class, but instead go to the teacher and ask for some private help. The student obviously had reservations about the teacher's willingness to help, but finally agreed when Mr. Bishop offered to approach the teacher first.

"Kids!" Mr. Bishop snorted as he hung up. "He's holding onto a D by the skin of his teeth and he knows it. But he expects me to hold his hand for him."

"Maybe he feels you're the only one who cares," Michon offered. "Maybe he's testing you."

"How?"

"I'm not sure." She shrugged. "I was just thinking that teenagers look more like adults than children, but inside they're not as self-confident as they'd like people to think. When they wind up in a situation where they don't feel in control they like knowing someone's in their corner."

Mr. Bishop nodded. "You sound like you understand kids."

I think we're going to work out. Besides, you're going to make my wife awfully grateful. May I call you Michon? Please call me Harry. I hate Harold."

Michon laughed. "I hate being called Miss Lycan. When should I get in touch with you about what I need to do?"

"That's Chas's department. You wouldn't happen to be his girl friend, would you?"

Michon shook her head. "No," she said simply.

"Pity. That's one of the world's good men."

Michon was still thinking about what Harry Bishop had said as she dropped by a fast-food stand to treat herself with a soft drink following the meeting at the school. So he considered Chas a good man. That's what her instincts about Chas had said.

Michon sat at a small table outside the stand, sipping her cool drink, letting everything sink in. She stared at her hands, noting the slight tremor to them. What was she thinking of? A canoe trip down the John Day River! What insanity had prompted her to talk to Harry? *You're scared to death, aren't you old girl?* she admitted. *Paul is going to laugh you into the next county when he finds out, if he doesn't send the men in the white coats and butterfly nets after you. And your mother will probably have a heart attack. All she wants is for you to get married like normal women. Why can't you do that little thing for her?*

Michon already knew the answer to that. She wasn't married because she hadn't found the man she wanted to link her life with. A handsome face, healthy pocketbook, even someone capable of stilling her body's restless urges, wasn't enough.

Her man, the man she was looking for had to have

weren't very happy with me the other day. I don't think very much of your way of trying to get back at me."

"That isn't it at all," she tried, suddenly exhausted. What did it matter? Why should she try to explain things to a man who had no idea what was going on inside her? "Paul, I'm terribly restless these days. I feel as if I'm trying to crawl out of my skin. I need a change of scene, that's all."

"That's a poor excuse, if you want my opinion. Have you really thought about what you're doing? You have no business going down a river in a canoe. Do you have any idea how insane that sounds? You're going to kill yourself or at least break one of those fingernails you're so proud of."

"To hell with my fingernails!" Michon snapped, surprised at the words coming from her mouth. "There have to be more important things in life than long fingernails."

"Like what?"

Like finding out why I'm so dissatisfied with my life, Michon thought, but she didn't tell Paul that. It would only start another endless circle of talk leading nowhere. Paul simply couln't understand that she could be filled with a nameless restlessness, and Michon no longer cared enough to try to spell it out for him. Besides, what was inside her was feelings, not words. "Paul, I have to hang up now," she said, realizing how final her words were. "Worthless needs his dinner."

Paul spat out something unkind about her dog and slammed down the receiver. Michon felt no tears as she turned away from the phone.

In fact Paul barely crossed her mind from then until the time, three days later, when she was back at the

wouldn't know you from Adam unless you'd gotten in touch with him. I had no idea I'd done such a good sales job on the John Day."

"You disapprove?" Michon asked. She was learning that leaving her face free of powder and blusher allowed her emotions to register with more intensity. She wasn't sure she was ready to give him that close a look at her thoughts. It felt so good to see him again! Did her expression register that?

Chas shrugged under the skintight T-shirt bearing the words CARSON CANOES. "Who am I to approve or disapprove? Your arrangement is with Harry and the school."

Michon cringed slightly under the terse sentences but managed to shrug off her thoughts. "You know, when you think about it, this is really all your fault. If you hadn't told me about canoeing I'd still be dying of boredom at a nine-to-five job."

"Oh, no, you don't." Chas was studying the fastenings on the life vest he held. "I'm not taking responsibility for this insanity of yours. I don't understand, but this isn't the time to talk about it. Well, did you come here to talk or work?"

"Work," Michon said spiritedly and then faltered. What did they expect her to do? She wouldn't be able to tell a good life vest from one ready for the dump. None of them looked comfortable. "Where did those come from?" she asked in a blatant attempt at stalling.

Harry explained that these belonged to the students, but not all of the vests were going to be allowed on the trip. "They have to be Coast Guard approved," he added. "The school's nervous enough about liability without our adding to their headaches. Come on, Chas. We

city girl like yourself want to live with spiders in your
sleeping bag, bugs trying to climb into the canoe, and
the possibility of a bear taking off with our food sup-
ply?''

"Do you think a spider or bug is going to send me
screaming through the woods? I don't happen to fit in
with that outdated stereotype,'' Michon said as she
found herself a place to perch on Harry's desk. She
swung her legs lazily. "Even we city women face a
spider or two in our lifetimes.'' She didn't mention that
the thought of a bear gave her a lot more pause than an
insect did. "I happen to be the only woman in my college biology class to volunteer to feed the two boa con-
strictors.''

"Congratulations,'' Chas said shortly, but Michon
thought she detected a note of respect in his voice.

In an effort to change the topic to something that
wouldn't set off sparks Michon asked Harry for infor-
mation about the teenagers who would be making up
the expedition. Harry explained that the twenty students were equally divided between boys and girls.
"Most of them plan to be physical education majors, so
they're in top shape physically. Unfortunately they're
also of the opinion that they know everything. It seems
to go with the territory. Getting them to listen can be a
real job.'' He smiled. "Kids think they have the world
by the tail. It takes a few years as members of the
school of hard knocks before they learn that they don't
know as much as they think they do.''

Michon nodded in understanding. "That sounds fa-
miliar,'' she laughed. "When I was eighteen I thought I
knew so much more than my folks that I must have
been impossible to live with. I was going to get married

turning the conversation back to the students. And yet, even as Harry described several self-confident jocks and a couple of girls bent on proving that they were as competent as any man on earth, Michon couldn't help but compare Paul with the teacher's description. Had she and Paul ever been able to communicate about anything important? Did he respect her, or was she simply the window dressing he needed during this stage of his life?

The answer didn't really matter. Paul was no longer part of what she was doing, would be doing. She was moving on. To what? She didn't have the answer to that, but it didn't bother her. The search was enough for now.

An hour later Harry had answered all her questions about the students, and Chas had given her a basic list of the supplies she would be expected to bring with her. At her admission that she owned neither waterproof boots nor a rain poncho, Chas offered to lend her some he had at his place. He seemed to have mellowed a little in the past hour. At least he no longer acted as if she had no business being in the room. "I'll try to remember to bring them to you in the next day or so," he said.

"Maybe I could come by your place and pick them up," Michon offered. "I don't want you to have to make unnecessary trips. You've got enough to do."

"If you want," Chas said, and gave her the address of his house in Shady Cove, a small town situated in the hills near the Rogue River. "It'll give you the opportunity to see a true bachelor's cabin."

"With spiders?"

"Of course," he shot back. "Probably a wolf pack prowling around the door. I'll try to beat them off."

warmth of his body, his breath on her hair, the sensation of jeans brushing against slacks. The dark corridor stretched ahead of them. If she could will it, there would be no end to the passageway.

facilities. I think tourists trying the Rogue River are what keeps it from turning into a ghost town.''

"I had relatives who lived there once,'' Traci said. "They lasted almost two years before my aunt said she'd sooner starve than stay there one more winter. They have a lot of snow and the roads get pretty bad. I wonder what people do in the winter. Probably go into hibernation.''

"Not Chas," Michon said, and explained about Chas's involvement with search-and-rescue.

"Sounds like you've got a real frontiersman on your hands," Traci giggled. "He doesn't eat with his fingers or anything, does he? I can just see him with a coonskin cap perched on his head while he eats. Feet on the table too."

"Hardly," Michon protested. She would have felt affronted if she didn't understand her friend's harmless teasing. "Just because he doesn't know why a place like Chantilla exists doesn't mean he's a savage."

"I didn't say he was. Look, if you like the guy, who am I to find fault? I just can't see the two of you having that much in common, that's all."

"Well we do—" Michon started and then stopped. What, really, did she and Chas Carson have in common? "At least we will if I survive this John Day River expedition," she said hopefully. "I hope I know what I'm getting myself into. Sometimes I think I'm crazy. It's too late to back down now."

"Were you thinking of backing down?"

"Of course not," Michon said with more conviction than she felt. The truth was, ever since her meeting with Harry and Chas she'd been honestly trying to face

scalp. "Four more days," she laughed over the sound of the car radio. "Four more days and no more panty hose!"

It took over an hour for Michon to reach Shady Cove. The drive on the two-lane road that traveled through farmland and reached up into the foothills was slowed by loaded logging trucks, campers, and trailers, none of them concerned with the thought that some people might be in a hurry to reach their destination.

The sign hanging over the town of Shady Cove was weather-beaten and in need of repair, but that didn't lower Michon's expectations. She stopped at the first service station and asked directions to the road Chas lived on.

"You looking for Carson Canoes?" the middle-aged man in the grease-stained coveralls asked. "That's about the only place on the road. You'll see his sign right off the highway, but it's another mile up to his place. He's the best guide in this state. He'll do right by you."

Michon said thanks and got back into her car. She drove through the town until she reached the outer town limits and then started looking for Chas's sign. It wasn't hard to locate, a small well-maintained sign on a wooden replica of a paddle. Michon made a mental note to ask Chas if she was right in her guess that he had both designed and made the sign. It ran the risk of being lost in a sea of neon signs, but there was something stable and honest about it that probably appealed to potential clients.

The station attendant was right. There weren't any other houses on the packed-earth-and-gravel road weaving itself through the hills and evergreens. As the hill

ing and started up the stairs leading to the spacious wraparound porch. There were no splinters on the railing and yet she could feel the uneven surface that existed because the wood hadn't had the life sanded out of it. The smell of warm wood penetrated her nostrils.

As Michon reached the porch level the large solid wood door opened. Chas stood in the doorway in his uniform of work shirt and jeans. His hair was uncombed, adding to his mountain-man appearance. For a moment she stared up at him. This was a man. Did he think of her as a woman? She had to fight off the impulse to touch him.

"It's magnificient," Michon whispered. "Did you build it?"

"That's a long story," Chas said as he led her inside. "I was a punk kid when this place was built. I've done the finishing work, but I'm not responsible for the basic house. The owner, a retired logger, hired me to do some of the more exciting aspects of the job, such as run to the hardware store for supplies, clean up after the men, and groom and feed the Clydesdales."

"Do what?" Michon had been torn between listening to Chas and trying to take in the magnificient open interior with its six-feet-long windows, and spiral staircase built in the center of the room and leading to the exposed second story.

"Clydesdales. They're a breed of draft horses."

"I know what they are. What do they have to do with building a log home?"

"A great deal, Miss Lycan. A great deal. Can I get you some coffee or something?"

Michon gave him a grateful smile, feeling somehow special because of his simple gesture. "Iced tea if you

ages, but there wasn't. He was just there whenever we needed him. He taught me everything I know about the mountains." Chas fastened his eyes on hers. "He taught me how to love the wilderness. When he died he left this house to me."

"Chas, that's beautiful." Michon sighed, feeling as if they were the only two people on earth at this moment, and loving the feeling. Did there have to be a past, a future? Now was enough. "He must have been a special man."

"He was." Chas was playing with his glass, his fingers idly rubbing against the icy surface, but his eyes were on her. "He never had any children of his own. It's sad, because he would have made a good father. I was pretty messed up after my dad died, but Bear pulled me back into line." Chas laughed softly. "He took me over his knee more than once. I never told my mother that. It was something between Bear and me. He was always setting goals for me, pushing me. He had an instinct for knowing what I was ready for. I just wish he were still here."

For several minutes Michon didn't feel any need to break the silence. Instead she found herself trying to picture Chas as a teenager trailing after a huge bear of a man who believed that kids should learn to whittle, be able to identify the sounds each bird makes, have the foresight to lay in enough wood to last the longest winter. Wasn't that more important that giving him money to play video games? "You said you were in charge of his horses," she said finally.

"He used them for horse logging," Chas explained as he leaned back in his sturdy chair. "Bear made his living logging, but he believed in preserving the forest

Michon could hardly call the room's contents junk. A bookshelf rose to the ceiling on one side, while an ancient but perfectly preserved rolltop desk dominated the opposite side. Photographs of an elk, a bear at the edge of a river, a sunset, and a flock of birds silhouetted against the sky took up another wall. Chas was rummaging through one of several boxes stacked in a corner. Finally he held up a pair of rubber-soled shoes. "They might fit after all," he said as he stared at Michon's feet.

Michon perched on the chair that accompanied the desk and started to remove her shoes. "Now that's what I call useful pack-ratting. How many men have in their possession a pair of women's all-weather shoes?"

"The owner never came back for them."

Something in Chas's tone stopped Michon. She stared at him, one of her tennis shoes dangling loosely in her hand. Chas's features were innocent enough, but his eyes had turned black, as if he were dropping a curtain over anything they might reveal. "Her loss is my gain," Michon said, not at all sure she was saying the right thing. "How long have they been hanging around here? Maybe she'll want them back."

"She won't. Try them on. I'll try to find that rain parka."

Michon had no choice but to respect Chas's back. She slipped her foot into the shoe, feeling more than a little uneasy because it was a perfect fit. She wasn't sure telling Chas that was the right thing. Nor was she sure she liked knowing how much she had in common with the nameless woman who was part of Chas's past. She was tying the heavy leather laces when Chas turned back toward her.

relationship between Chas and April hadn't been that deep. Clearly she meant a great deal to him, and her leaving had opened wounds which had not yet healed. There were a few touches, like hanging plants and the quilt on his bed that made Michon wonder if April had lived there with Chas.

A minute later Chas was leading her into his bedroom. The air of masculinity surrounding it was unmistakable—and disturbing. Rich deep-chocolate carpeting picked up the wood tones of the handmade bedstead and the brown in the painstakingly sewn bedspread. The closet door was pulled back to reveal a row of flannel work shirts and wool jackets. Michon spotted a conservative suit encased in clear plastic, but imagined it seldom saw use. More of Chas's outdoor photographs graced the paneled walls.

"I feel like I'm in a den," Michon observed. "This is definitely a man's room."

"Do you disapprove?"

"How could I disapprove?" Michon turned toward him, puzzled. "It's your house. You have every right to do with it what you want. Actually I think it complements the log construction perfectly. And it reflects what I know of your personality."

"Then I was wrong about you," Chas said as he settled himself casually on the bed. "I didn't think this place would fit your style at all."

"You didn't?" She felt hurt. She wasn't at all like the woman he saw that first day. "Chas, I've seen so many modern apartments that I'm sick to death of them. I'll never understand why condominiums are so popular. This place—this place says something about its owner."

fought it off. It wasn't right. Not yet. "You're talking about April, aren't you?" she ventured. "She keeps coming up in your conversations."

"I'll try to remedy that."

"Don't," Michon protested. "If you want to talk about her, talk." Stop, a small voice cried as something vulnerable inside Michon admitted that the topic would bring her pain.

"I don't. April belongs to the past." Chas opened his eyes and stared deep into Michon's. "At least I learned one thing from the experience. I'm not going to ever give that much of myself again."

"Because it hurt too much?" Michon ventured. No. This wasn't what she wanted to talk about.

Instead of answering, Chas only stared at Michon, his eyes dark, the young-boy quality in him replaced by age. Finally he sighed. "I'm turning over a new leaf, or at least I'm taking a shot at it. I've been pretty serious about life so far. I've always pushed myself, tried to be the best I can be. I can't change that, but I've learned that serious relationships run the risk of backlash. From now on I intend to enjoy what happens. But I'm keeping my emotions out of it."

"I don't see how you can do that," Michon whispered, supressing a shudder because it upset her to hear Chas talk like that. She was reacting to him. She wanted to know that he was capable of the same feeling. "Humans aren't able to keep their emotions out of their relationships with people."

"Don't worry, Michon. It can be done."

Michon started to shake her head, but Chas didn't give her the opportunity to continue. He reached over, pulled her toward him until she was stretched out be-

He had enough self-control to hold his emotions in check. His kiss might be no more than a physical act on his part, but there was enough of the code of the gentleman in him to make her feel safe, even in his remote home.

Outside two birds called back and forth to each other, ticking off the seconds, as Michon gave herself totally to the emotion of the moment. In saner times she might have never agreed to come here, but that was before Chas had walked into her life and challenged her with his reality, made her face the fact that she was a woman with all the needs, emotions, and reactions of a woman.

Michon wouldn't have objected if Chas had touched her breasts, made their contact more intimate than it was, but he didn't. Instead he simply kissed her, a gentle kiss that reached her soul. Her own personal code of right and wrong wasn't tested. Their kiss was a simple act and carried no threat of taking the relationship at a faster, potentially dangerous pace.

At last the kiss ended. Chas held her away from him, his eyes searching her features, for what, she didn't know. "Why did you come here?"

"To—to get some shoes."

"Is that all?"

"No." Michon fought to pull herself back from that suspended state Chas had so effortlessly placed her in. "I—there's something we have to talk about." She sat up, putting necessary distance between them. "When we were with Harry I had the distinct feeling that you weren't happy with me. It was as if you could barely stand to be in the same room with me. Chas, you don't really want me on this trip, do you?"

"Not in so many words. But you're thinking it, aren't you? I might ask the same thing of you, Chas," Michon said sharply, her mood now wary and bordering on anger. "After all, what happened on this bed a minute ago isn't what happens between casual friends."

"I'm sorry about that." Chas was now massaging her wrist, as if wordlessly soothing away any discomfort he might have inflicted on her. "That kiss was for me. We were talking about emotions, specifically my emotions. Let's call it a test and leave it at that." Chas surged to his feet and paced to the window. He stood motionless for a moment and then whirled back toward Michon. "What if we lay off the serious conversation for now. Whatever reasons you have for getting Harry to take you on, they're your reasons."

"Thank you." Michon was trembling slightly under the intensity of his stare, afraid she wasn't hiding her emotions well. Should she walk away from this complex man? Life would be much smoother without him disrupting it.

"There's just one thing that needs to be open between us," he continued. "I meant what I said about wanting to keep my emotions out of the relationship I have with people."

Why? Michon thought. *How did April hurt you so much?*

But she kept her questions to herself. She wasn't sure she'd be able to keep her senses about her through further talk. Chas might have kissed her only to prove that she had no effect on him. Michon couldn't say the same about her own emotions.

didn't. The other day, when I went to his place, he kissed me. We were sitting on his bed and he kissed me. I felt it clear down to my toes. Well''—Michon giggled self-consciously—''maybe it wasn't my toes.''

"Just kissed?" Traci's expression showed that she had her doubts.

"Yes. At least I'm sure that's how he saw it.''

"And now you're afraid you won't be able to keep your dignity around him when you're snuggled into sleeping bags under a full moon.'' Traci took another sip of wine, a slight grin tugging at her lips. "My dear, don't you know what a perfect situation you've got going for you? Okay, so the jock, your mountain man, whatever you want to call him, he wants to play handshaking acquaintances. Do you think he's going to feel that way by the time this little trip is over? Look, the two of you are going to be spending days and days, to say nothing of nights, together. Anything can happen.''

"No.'' Michon stifled a moan and reached for her wineglass. "He still loves this April. I don't know what she did to him, but it must have been something earth-shattering. He isn't interested in another woman. He's been hurt. I don't know what to do about it.''

"Don't sell yourself short, my friend. You don't have to go around covered by burlap. You're not that hard on the eyes.''

"That's not what I want.'' Michon sat cross-legged on the rug and snapped her fingers to let Worthless know he could come over for some attention. "I'm not interested in some quick romance. Casual sex isn't my cup of tea. Oh, darn, I don't know what I want. But it isn't a one-night stand.'' Michon blushed. "Forget I said that. I've never had a one-night stand in my life.

Worthless with her, even though that meant caring for a dog while making last minute preparations for a wedding. Traci even offered to drop by the apartment to water Michon's plants. "Just don't drown or something," Traci teased. "I'd be willing to adopt Worthless, but I'm afraid your poor mutt would pine away to nothing if you were gone very long."

Michon scratched Worthless behind the ear. "Poor baby. You don't understand what's happening, do you? Believe me, I'd like to take you with me but I'm afraid the John Day River isn't the place for a dog."

"Maybe you can take a homing pigeon with you and send him back here with a message for Worthless," Traci suggested. "You sure as heck aren't going to be able to use a telephone out there. I still can't believe you're doing it. The city girl is really heading for the boondocks. Your grandfather would be proud of you."

Boondocks certainly described the country Michon found herself in the next day. She'd driven over to the high school before dawn, loaded her belongings into the school bus that the school district had loaned the expedition, and climbed into the bus along with Harry and the students. Harry explained that Chas would be meeting the group at Service Creek with the canoes late in the afternoon. Michon was kept on her toes getting to know the students, particularly the girls. She'd been worried that the students would consider her an outsider and have as little as possible to do with her, but they'd been on the road only a few minutes before Michon found herself joining the animated conversations. Talk was of a general nature for the first few hours. It wasn't until they were bouncing along quiet country

only hope that Chas didn't guess that she hadn't been able to shake off his impact on her. Yes, he'd accused her of using the expedition as an excuse to continue to be around him, but she hoped he believed that the air had been cleared between them and they'd function simply as two adults, with the safety and education of the students as their one common bond. Whether he held that belief was something only time would tell.

"Is this what you expected?" Harry asked as he joined her beside the pile of belongings that had been unpacked beside the bus at the end of the journey.

For the second time since getting off the bus Michon took the opportunity to take in her surroundings. The barren, harsh desert terrain seemed an unlikely location for a river. Little in the way of plant life grew on the wind-sculptured hills, and what little sage and wild grass had managed to find a toehold was more gray than green, as if lacking in some essential nutrients plants need from the soil. The Service Creek Store they'd passed on their way to the campsite had struck Michon as a quiet, sometimes lonely, way for someone to make a living. She couldn't help but wonder if the store supplied anyone other than visitors to the John Day River, although Harry had said something about there being a few ranchers in the area. What they could raise or grow Michon had no idea, although she had visions of rangy, wild cattle, and sheep with their coats matted with burrs, managing to stay alive only because their natural food was supplemented with hay by their owners. She wasn't sure she'd ever want to live in an area this remote, but the contrast to the city atmosphere was like a shot of adrenalin. She lifted her head, drinking in the dry, clean, sage-saturated air.

first time since she'd met him, Chas was wearing sunglasses. His faded T-shirt and cut-offs were the only signs Michon needed to tell her that his truck wasn't air-conditioned. Michon had never considered a man's legs to be his best feature, but she couldn't keep her eyes off the knotted cords of muscle defining Chas's calves and thighs. The softly curled hairs were light and just thick enough to finish the picture of a mature male. Obviously he kept himself in physical condition for the work he did.

Harry and the boys hurried over to help Chas unload, but Michon held back. Was she ready for this? Now that it was too late to turn back, Michon found herself thinking of her warm, clean apartment, her soft bed, her safe, if boring, relationship with Paul.

What she shared with Chas wasn't safe. Even if he didn't want it discussed, she was all too aware of her reactions to him. It wasn't going to be easy to keep up her end of the guidelines he'd spelled out—a relationship without involvement of the emotions. But it was what he wanted, what he believed in. She had no choice but to try to follow his rules.

"We'll use tonight to test our skills at setting up and taking down camp," Harry explained to the assembled group, once the ground near him was covered with the equipment needed by the expedition. "I already know how some of you feel about not being able to bring tents, but as you can guess by the look of the land, it doesn't rain here very often. It's going to get cold at night, which is why all of you were told to bring the heaviest sleeping bags you could get your hands on. There will be a certain amount of discomfort because we won't be using tents, but on the other hand we

up in the water because they're expendable when you're trying to keep from tipping over."

"Are we supposed to wear those rubber-soled boots?" Michon asked. "Really, they're not all that comfortable."

Chas fastened his eyes on Michon, but because he was still wearing his sunglasses she couldn't read anything in them. The wind was whipping his hair, lending an air of savagery to his appearance. "I'm sorry you don't like the boots, Miss Lycan. You may find they're the best friend you have. No, you don't have to wear them unless weather conditions warrant it. Tennis shoes will do fine. I hope you brought along more than one pair. I can almost guarantee that the ones you wear in the canoe will not be dry by the end of the day."

Michon reached into her pocket and pulled out the list Chas had given her. "Of course," she responded airily. "Your instructions were thorough. If I've forgotten anything it'll be my fault and not some oversight on your part."

"Thanks for the vote of confidence," Chas said, his mouth twitching again. "All right. One more thing. I've arranged with someone at the Service Creek Store to drive the truck and bus to Cottonwood Bridge, our takeout point. I'm afraid this is the last time we'll be looking at modern transportation until the trip is over. If anyone is having second thoughts, this is the time to tell me."

Chas's words made Michon shudder. It wasn't that she was afraid, just suddenly very conscious of how much she and the others would be dependent on Chas's skills until they reached Cottonwood Bridge. True, canoeing on the John Day wasn't the same as

girls were getting ready to warm up some chili that had been prepared ahead of time. It seemed a minor miracle to have a camp actually take shape with her help. Thank heavens for some camping experience!

Since by then the sun was hidden behind the mountains, Michon wandered off behind one of the low hills where she had the privacy to change from shorts into jeans and pull a sweat shirt over her head. A few minutes later she walked over to the sandy but rocky beach where Chas and several of the boys were getting the canoes ready to put in the water in the morning. Chas, too, had changed to long pants but was still wearing his well worn T-shirt. He was squatting over a red canoe, running his fingers over its hull. Michon stood behind him, content to watch the play of the wind in his tousled hair until one of the teenagers spotted her. "Which canoe do you want?" he asked.

"Good grief, I don't know," she admitted. "They all look the same to me."

Chas straightened and turned to her. If he was aware of the change from shorts to jeans he didn't show it. "They aren't," he said simply.

"I'd like to learn."

"Would you really? Come here. I'll give you a quick lesson." He pointed at a line of canoes resting upside down, their round-, flat-, and V- bottomed hulls exposed. "First, they're all about the same length. Most of mine run about sixteen feet. Two people and one hundred and fifty pounds of gear fit nicely in a sixteen-foot canoe."

"Are all of them for two people?" Michon asked, wondering despite herself if she'd be paired with Chas.

"Not necessarily. A lot depends on the canoeist's

to lighten the mood. "I'm going to be a klutz. At first."

"I won't laugh. However, I might not be above a little blackmail if you're a total klutz. A little under-the-table payoff, or I'll tell everyone how you almost drowned us."

"I haven't done it yet." Michon didn't move. Chas's hand was still on her shoulder, holding her securely within the force of his presence.

"True." His hand dropped from her shoulder to her wrist. He held her hand up in the air, studying her fingers. "You've gotten rid of the paint on your nails, but they're still too long. Those fingers of yours don't look very strong. Believe me, you're going to have blisters by the end of tomorrow. If I did blackmail you, how much are you worth? I figure I might as well get everything I can out of this."

Michon couldn't stifle a laugh. The change from Chas's previous serious approach to life delighted her. "Don't get your hopes too high. The best I could offer you are the keys to an unpaid car. I hardly think it's worth your trouble. I do have a dog but his name is Worthless. That describes his value to everyone except me."

"There go my dreams of instant wealth." Chas squeezed her hand briefly before turning to the canoes. "Which color tickles your fancy, milady? If we're going to risk our lives, we might as well do it in style."

Michon's hand was still tingling in reaction to Chas's squeeze as she pointed at one of two wooden crafts. "That one. I love wood."

Chas smiled. "That's the first canoe I ever owned. I've tried them all—aluminum, fiberglass, polyethy-

Michon stood back, watching as Chas demonstrated how to carry a canoe to the water by lifting it and rolling it over him until he had the center thwart resting on his shoulders. Once the canoe was in the river with Chas holding it in place, he explained that Michon was to grasp the gunwales on either side, step into the canoe, and lower herself into it with most of her weight on her arms, not her feet.

Michon grinned sheepishly, stepped toward the canoe and took a deep breath. Although the river edge was calm, she had the uneasy feeling that the craft would start rocking any moment. She was really going to do it! "Are you sure you're ready for this?" she asked, stalling for time. "My father thought I was never going to learn how to ride a bike."

"Get in," was all he said.

Michon followed his instructions religiously, relieved that her weight wasn't enough to lower the canoe more than a few inches as she dropped to her knees in the bottom of the craft. "Success!" she proclaimed and then caught her breath as Chas swung into the canoe and pushed it toward the middle of the river with a single fluid movement. "What are you doing? Where are we going?" she gasped, grabbing the canoe's gunwales on either side of her.

"Relax," Chas ordered as he handed her a maple paddle. "What you're getting tonight is known as the Carson crash course. Okay, lesson one. We need what's known as a well-trimmed canoe. That means it should be absolutely level in the water. Now, if you agree that I weigh more than you do, then you will probably agree that I shouldn't sit as close to the stern as you are to the bow. That's how we stay balanced."

shaft? Good girl. Now pay attention. It isn't complicated."

While Michon chewed on her lower lip in concentration, she struggled to follow Chas's instructions to lean forward at the waist and extend her arms. She felt the water lapping at her lower hand as she punched the paddle blade into the water, but didn't let that distract her. By using both arm and back muscles, she pulled the canoe forward. When the paddle was parallel with her hips she pulled it out of the water as Chas had directed.

"That wasn't so hard," she exclaimed after a few more tries.

"Piece of cake? Is that what you're thinking? Wait until you've done that for eight hours and then try to get up the next morning. I just hope you're limber, or your muscles are really going to be complaining."

"I won't complain," Michon said to the outline behind her in the dark.

"Why?" The question was asked almost too sharply.

Michon rose to the occasion. "Because I'm not a complainer. I never have been and I see no reason to begin now." She didn't try to explain that there'd always been something in her backbone that made her rise to every challenge and never admit it even when she was dangerously close to the end of her rope. It hadn't happened many times in her life, but she felt confident that she wouldn't lose her head in an emergency.

"I like that in a woman," Chas said. "I hope you can live up to your words."

Before Michon had time to respond to his challenge, Chas turned to teaching a new stroke, which he explained was used in quiet water when the canoeists needed a change of pace. That took longer for Michon to

Harry or one of the boys should be able to handle a canoe alone, at least for the first day."

She felt deflated. "Oh. Well, thank you. I guess."

"I just wish you'd had the training the others have," Chas said shortly. "I sure hope you can keep up."

"I will. I'm no quitter. I'll pull my own weight," Michon replied firmly, repeating her silent vow to maintain the group's pace no matter what the cost to herself physically. She had something to prove to Chas—and to herself. The hour she'd just spent in the canoe had cemented her resolve. She was going to see this John Day trip to its completion! It had become a point of honor with her, proof that she was more, much more, than a mannequin putting in her eight hours at Chantilla.

As they headed back to shore neither of them spoke. Chas gave her instructions on the proper way to bring a canoe to land and how to exit while the craft was still in the water. Despite her best effort, and despite the fact that Chas was kneeling in the sand holding onto the canoe, Michon misjudged the distance to shore and soaked her tennis shoes when she stepped out. She bit her lip, praying that he hadn't noticed her misstep in the dark.

"You're squishing," Chas observed. "Got your feet wet, did you?"

"I'm fine!" Michon retorted in an effort to cover up her embarrassment. "I'm not complaining."

"I didn't say anything about that, did I? I'm just making an observation. I suppose tennis shoes feel pretty foreign after wearing high heels all the time. I just hope you get a little more sure-footed before this is over."

pulse to rest her head against him, to close her eyes, and let this very special man lead her where he willed. Inside she felt herself melting, relaxing. She'd never felt like this around any other man. Maybe it was no more than their surroundings that allowed her mind to block off everything except the deeply pleasant sensation of caring about, thinking of nothing except, a warm male body, a cool breeze, her primitive response to him.

Someone had brought a guitar and was playing it softly for the assembled teenagers. There was a mutter of conversation, the play of firelight against the dark and barren cliffs. To Michon these impressions added up to a perfect whole. Chas had his arm around her. He was allowing her to touch him. The night was magic. She would think of nothing else.

me a few moments of yourself. She was all too aware that moments like they'd shared might not come again. She was also wise enough to enjoy them for what they were...isolated stretches of time to be savored but not mourned should they not be repeated.

Was she falling in love? Michon didn't have the answer to that question. If she had been eighteen she most likely would have replied yes, but in the years since she'd been a teenager, Michon had learned that the human heart was capable of producing the most complex emotions, none of which were incapable of being superseded. Today's great love could become tomorrow's memory. Trying to sort out the roots of those emotions usually led to a headache, tears in a pillow, and precious little else. She was old enough to know the wisdom of taking each day, each experience, as it came until the sum of those experiences was made clear to her. It was enough to know that she was supremely content to be around Chas, at the same time to be aware of his belief that emotions could be held in check.

That was what he wanted. She would accept that.

And if her heart was wounded in the process, that was the price she would have to pay. Heartache was an unavoidable human emotion. The alternative was to stay away from Chas. That was something she would not, could not, do.

Michon fell asleep thinking about the meal they'd shared sitting side by side on a rock, with the blaze from the campfire warming their cheeks and drying her shoes.

When the sounds of activity woke her, Michon realized that she had indeed slept through the night. She took a moment to record the occasion with her camera. The lens caught sun glinting off water, long morning-shadows, a sleek craft cutting knifelike through the smooth surface.

After she put her camera away Michon stood near Chas, feeling useless because she didn't have the skill to push off a loaded canoe and settle into it without upsetting everything, especially while wearing a life vest. She felt both grateful and embarrassed as he held the wooden canoe's gunwales firmly and directed her to step in, her weight squarely in the middle of the canoe. She barely suppressed a sigh of relief as she found her seat and waited for Chas to join her. At least she hadn't gotten her shoes wet yet.

Michon glanced around, grinning slightly in response to the excited looks on the students' faces. Only Harry seemed serious, almost preoccupied.

Chas dipped his paddle into the water and quickly moved to the front of the line of canoes. "We'll be going under the Service Creek Bridge," he called out. "Swing wide above the bridge. I'll show you the best path around the supports."

Michon took a deep if somewhat shaky breath and turned back to say a silent good-bye to last night's campsite, the last sign of civilization. The beach hadn't been Grand Central Station, but at least the little Service Creek Store was within walking distance. Now—now she didn't know what lay ahead. But Chas was with her. He was competent, in control. He didn't have to say it. The way he carried himself was enough to make her feel secure.

"There used to be a ferry here," Chas said as they passed under the bridge. "If I remember right, in the

been using," Chas explained. "I'll handle the fancy stuff. Just remember, the speed of the river determines our speed. I could slow our craft down and give you a greater sense of security but that's a heck of a lot more work. Since we won't have many obstacles to go around here, we might as well sit back and enjoy the ride."

That's easy for you to say, Michon thought but she held her tongue. If Chas was using the fast water ahead of them to test her, Michon was determined to do her best. She clamped her jaws together, took another look at the unrelenting landscape, and then stared ahead at the river pulling them along like a cable pulling a roller coaster up the initial climb. No matter how scared she might become, she wasn't going to let Chas know.

The canoe started to pick up speed. She could feel Chas sweeping them to the left, but she didn't dare take her eyes off the river long enough to glance back at him. Her stomach lurched slightly as she became aware of how quickly the landscape was passing behind them. Michon gripped her paddle tighter, knuckles white, remembering only intermittently to dip the paddle into the water. Why should she? They were going quite fast enough, thank you!

Then, almost abruptly, their pace slowed. Michon forced her hands to relax their grip and leaned back until she was once again sitting instead of kneeling. She took a grateful breath, waiting for her heart to stop pounding in her chest.

"Nothing to it. Piece of cake, isn't it?" Chas asked.

"I didn't squeal," she pointed out when she could trust herself to talk. "Are there many more rapids like that?"

"We got wet. That's all."

"You were in the canoe? Who was with you?" He had too much skill for the kind of accident he'd described. What had happened?

"April. She panicked."

Michon closed her eyes tightly against the current of emotion that coursed unchecked through her. The last time Chas had been on the river April had been with him. No! Why hadn't she known that? It was bad enough knowing that Chas still carried the memory of April with him. Why did the woman and what she meant to Chas have to be tied up with the journey she was undertaking with Chas? "I'm sorry," she managed after a lengthy silence. "I didn't mean to bring that up."

"You didn't know. Forget it."

Again silence settled down over the small canoe. Michon tried to concentrate on the landscape, the contours of the river, but her thoughts kept filling with snatches of what she felt sure was going through Chas's mind too. The sense of adventure, the tug of fear at the back of Michon's mind, had been replaced by depression. She didn't want April in the canoe with them!

But April couldn't be avoided. Someday, somehow, the past would have to be brought into the open. Darn April for doing what she'd done to him!

Michon had shaken off enough of her depression to be searching for a conversation topic when Chas spoke. "You might want to get out your camera in a few minutes," he said as if they'd never spoken a serious word to each other. "We're going to be passing some old buildings that were built around the turn of the century. The ranchers used to raise sheep and cattle and

"April didn't like it. She was afraid there were rats living in the old house."

"Rats? I didn't think about that." Michon refused to mention April.

"She was right, unfortunately for her. They're probably still in the barn because of the feed stored there. At least they were when we were here."

Michon laughed, determined to place April in the past, giving her the necessary push to continue the conversation. "Well, when you think about it, they have first rights. After all, they've been here a lot longer than we have. If humans are willing to build them some shelters, why shouldn't the rats take advantage of things? Are we going to stop here?" she asked. "We've only been in the water a little while."

"No," Chas answered as the landscape flowed by. "The only reason we stopped here before was that we'd had trouble with that one canoe capsizing. Everything got wet and I had to patch the canoe." Chas shook his head as Michon glanced at him. "I've never seen April so upset."

"Why?" A moment before she'd been determined not to mention April, but she had to admit that ignoring her presence on the river wasn't going to make her go away.

"April likes things predictable. She didn't handle the upset very well. She was pretty shook-up."

So simple. Chas's explanation was so cut-and-dried, and yet it left too much unsaid. Was this why April was no longer part of Chas's life, or was there more to the story than anger? "The memories here aren't very pleasant, are they?" she ventured.

Michon sensed rather than saw Chas shake his head.

At Michon's prompting, Chas told her a little more of the country's history including the origin of names of the area's landmarks.

Conversation took a backseat when Chas and Michon reached a sharp right bend in the river. Michon's muscles tensed and she ground her teeth together in concentration as he directed her through the moves needed to maneuver the canoe through the turn without letting it get close to some fallen brush half-submerged in the moving water. Michon learned that back ferrying was another word for putting the canoe in reverse and back paddling to keep to the inside of the bend. "Why didn't you tell me about this before?" Michon gasped as she struggled to keep the canoe away from branches reaching out to snag the canoe should it drift too close.

"Sorry," Chas called back. "But this is something you can only learn by doing. Don't tell me you're complaining. You're the one who wanted the great adventure."

"I'm not complaining," she said, without letting her eyes stray from the river or the path she was imagining for the craft. Her fingers ached and the muscles between her shoulder blades were tense, but she wasn't going to tell him. "I'm just glad we're not traveling any faster."

"We're barely crawling. Have you ever seen a white-water race? That's what you'd call moving."

Michon waited until the bend was behind them before responding to Chas's question. "I don't even know what you mean by a white-water race. I take it that's something you've done."

"Yep. There's no experience like it. I'll tell you

between her shoulders, and repositioned her legs. Her fingers tingled, both from the pressure they were being subjected to and from a primitive ache to run them up the inside of the shirt that fit Chas like a glove.

Did he have any idea how desirable, how animallike he looked at this moment? Michon found herself blushing slightly, but not enough to try to stop her thoughts. If a man was capable of shedding his civilized skin and becoming one with the river and the craft under him, this was what Chas was doing at this moment. He was as much a part of the John Day as boulders and white water and deep, quiet pools. There was only one way of expressing Michon's reaction.

You're sexy. You're a sexy, desirable man. And I want you! God, at this moment I want you.

As Harry pulled alongside Michon she clamped a violent lid on her emotions and pulled the cloak of civilization back over her features. Desire wasn't an emotion to share with outsiders. What she still felt inside she hoped didn't show in her eyes.

"How's it going?" Harry asked, his lips a tight line that bothered her. "You need any liniment?"

"Probably tonight. My hands are kind of sore," Michon admitted. "Right now, though, I feel as if I could do this forever. I think I'm turned on to this old river."

"You haven't seen Russo Rapids yet," Chas warned. "Just don't panic on me, okay?"

I won't, Michon vowed silently. *I'm going to pass this test. You're here. Nothing can go wrong.*

But when they reached Russo Rapids, Michon wasn't quite so sure. Her opinion of Chas hadn't changed, only her own self-confidence. They'd passed the area where a man had lived for twenty years in a dugout, and Shofly

that the life jacket was covering her, but knew that when the time came to remove the jacket, her body would be sharply outlined under the wet garment.

Would Chas respond? From the way he was concentrating on guiding the others through Russo Rapids she couldn't be sure. He was, after all, the leader of the expedition. He had more important matters on his mind than the decency or indecency of her appearance. But she wanted him to notice. She wouldn't deny that.

By the time the group was under way again, Michon had become aware of the wind's growing force. She looked up, surprised to find the sun high in the sky. She began to wonder how much more wind they would have to contend with before they were ready to leave the river. Chas, however, seemed unconcerned about that. He'd launched into another of his seemingly endless stories about the history of the John Day. "See those flat-topped rocks up ahead?" he asked. "That's Squaw Butte. It's named after some Indian who had five squaws. He was quite a hunter and kept them busy tanning his hides. The story goes that the squaws wanted to go to the Columbia and kept nagging him about it. He turned his horses loose so they couldn't leave."

"Sounds like slave labor to me," Michon observed.

"Sounds like good thinking to me," Chas said, a wink giving away his true feelings. "He wasn't going to make his fortune if he lost his labor force."

"He probably paid dearly for it," she laughed. "Can you imagine trying to keep five wives happy?"

"I can't imagine keeping one woman happy. If there's a knack to it, I sure haven't found it."

sake of a customer, or think ahead to her evening's plans.

For the balance of the afternoon Michon wasn't aware of consciously thinking of anything. She soaked in impressions and sensations without concentrating on them. Her eyes acted like a camera, recording what she was seeing and filing it for future reference. She nibbled on an apple when Chas handed it to her, and when they passed close to the shoreline, she tossed out the core, hoping that some bird or small animal would find her offering to the creatures who made their home here.

"One more mile to go," Chas said after a lengthy silence. "Think you can make it?"

"What? Of course," Michon replied, rousing herself with an effort. "I feel like I've been in this canoe half of my life."

"Be patient. It won't be much longer."

"That's okay. I feel as if I could do this forever. I don't care about anything else."

"You mean it? Not many people say that. Maybe you can handle this after all."

Was that meant as a compliment? Michon struggled momentarily to find the answer, but her mind refused to focus on any serious questions. She was content to surrender her body to the craft's rhythmic swaying, to battle the constant wind. *I'd make a good machine*, she thought. *Just plug me in and I can drift along all day*. Even Chas's pointing out an old cabin and mentioning that a drowning had taken place not far from the Twickenham Bridge years ago failed to give her anything worth concentrating on.

Michon had been staring at Twickenham Bridge for

shore and then walked slowly over to where she was rubbing her aching knees. "Are you all right?" he asked as he knelt beside her.

His unexpected concern, when she was sure she deserved some comment about her not being in shape for the journey, was all it took to push Michon over the edge. She dropped her head and buried her face in the protection of her hands. Tears she didn't understand but didn't try to stop wracked her slender form. She was vaguely aware of Chas rubbing her back between the shoulder blades, but in her present state there wasn't enough of her left over emotionally to respond.

"What are you crying for?" Chas asked, his hands still providing their healing therapy. "Is it what happened earlier, about April?"

Michon shook her head. Her voice broke several times as she spoke. "I'm sorry. I had no right saying what I did. I don't know what existed between you and April." She looked up at him through tear-blurred eyes. "That's the trouble. I don't know what happened and what it did to you."

"You're right. You don't. Look, you're tired, wrung out. Actually"—he paused dramatically and then winked— "you're not quite up to being hired as a sea captain yet, but you've got promise. At least you're no quitter."

Michon felt her tears stop as the other canoes came to shore and the students started walking over to where she was sitting. With a shaky sigh Michon wiped her eyes and busied herself with removing her life jacket. The fabric under the jacket was soaked, and despite her efforts to dislodge her cotton blouse, it continued to cling tightly to her breasts and rib cage. Her bra did

Worthless had trusted her instinctively from the moment she first picked him up. Was this how her body was responding to Chas?

Slowly, almost shyly, Chas placed his hands on her shoulders and held her back from him as if studying a painting he was considering buying. She trembled, met his eyes, and lost herself in their depths. "You're a beautiful woman, Michon," he whispered.

Harlequin reaches
into the hearts and minds
of women across America
to bring you

Harlequin American Romance.™

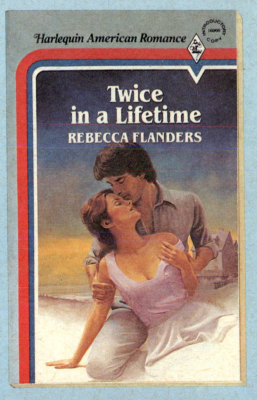

Get this
Book and
Tote Bag
FREE!

MAIL TO:
Harlequin Reader Service
2504 West Southern Avenue
Tempe, Arizona 85282

YES! I want to discover *Harlequin American Romance*. Send me FREE and without obligation, "Twice in a Lifetime" and my FREE tote bag. If you do not hear from me after I have examined my FREE book, please send me the 4 new *Harlequin American Romance* novels each month as soon as they come off the presses. I understand that I will be billed only $2.25 per book (total $9.00). There are no shipping or handling charges. There is no minimum number of books that I have to purchase. In fact, I may cancel this arrangement at any time. "Twice in a Lifetime" and the tote bag are mine to keep as FREE gifts even if I do not buy any additional books.

154 CIA NAYA

Name	(Please Print)	
Address		Apt. No.
City	State/Prov.	Zip/Postal Code

Signature (If under 18, parent or guardian must sign.)

ARIPT384

were going to go on strike if they weren't shown a little respect. Michon had to laugh. Their spirits revived her own. In fact being with the teenagers was giving her a fresh zest for life, one she knew she would deeply miss when the journey was over.

"Men!" a small but wiry seventeen-year-old named Shanna said to Michon. "We're good enough to keep up our end of the paddling all day, but look how fast those dumb boys fall back into old habits. Women's lib, my eye! The only thing they care about is their bellies. What manual says we have to cook while they sit on their duffs?"

"How far do you think you'll get if you tell them that?" Michon asked, knowing the answer already. "Do you think they'd have dinner before you starved?"

"I'd probably starve," Shanna shrugged philosophically. "That's okay," she went on, lowering her voice. "I knew what I was doing when I got in Skip's canoe. Sometimes a girl has to take the initiative. After dinner I think I'm going to suggest that we take a walk. Just so we know what the country looks like around here, right? Did you see the moon and stars last night? Fantastic! If that doesn't give him ideas, then he's a lost cause."

"You like him, do you?" Michon was pretty sure that Skip was the skinny boy with a smattering of freckles on his cheeks.

Shanna grinned. "I like him. Some of these guys think they're God's gift to women, but Skip's not like that. He's easy to talk to. I'll tell you what. If I promise to keep Skip away from that hill ahead of us, maybe you can get Chas to take you there."

brought enough? Fresh air must put appetites in high gear," she said. "We might have to take up hunting or fishing if this bunch isn't going to starve."

"They sure can eat, can't they? Michon, you wouldn't have any liniment on you would you?"

Michon speared a tomato slice. "As a matter of fact, that's one of the items Chas suggested. It's in my bag. Don't tell me I'm not the only one to be feeling the effects of our day."

Harry smiled, but Michon thought she detected a certain tightness around the corners of his mouth. "I confess. Only, in my case, I'm afraid it's a little more than sore muscles."

"Are you all right?" Michon asked, concerned. She now noticed that Harry was eating slowly with his left hand while holding his shoulders at an awkward angle. He was shivering slightly, but still wearing his wet shirt.

"Just old age, my dear." Harry smiled his wan smile again. "It's bursitis. I had a shot of some anesthetic for it before we took off, but I'm afraid it isn't doing the job. Be glad you're young."

"I'm sorry. You're in pain, aren't you? Hold on. I'll show you what I brought." Michon started to get up, but Harry stopped her.

"Indulge me, will you?" he whispered. "I'd just as soon the others didn't see you playing nurse for me. Chas asked more than once if I was in shape for this. I assured him that I was. I just hope I'm right. I don't want him to have any more on his mind than necessary. You understand, don't you?"

Michon wasn't sure she did, but she agreed to keep quiet, at least for the time being. As they finished their meal Harry explained that he'd ignored the growing

used to do a lot of this survival business, but that was years ago. I guess I had to prove to myself that I wasn't ready for a rocking chair yet. Maybe when you're older, you'll understand what I'm talking about."

Michon put down her plate, took Harry's hands in hers and squeezed them gently. She felt closer to Harry than she dreamed possible. "I know exactly what you're talking about," she whispered, her throat tight. "Why do you think I'm here?"

"Because Chas is a one-of-a-kind guy, and you're interested."

Michon blushed but shook off Harry's words. "Let's not talk about that, okay? I'm here because I don't want to be a grandmother some day with nothing more to tell my grandchildren than how I went to Seattle on a buying trip for a store so expensive I couldn't afford to shop there myself. My grandchildren couldn't care less about that. I want to look back on this experience someday and say, 'Hey, I did it!'"

Harry gave her a broad grin and a wink. "You and I think a lot alike, Michon. I had a good feeling about you from the start. Look, about that liniment, if you don't mind, I think I'll borrow it later. I was going to pack some, but my wife was watching. Damn pride!"

"Harry?" Michon ventured. "I think we should tell Chas. He might want you in his canoe where he can help you. I'm sure he's going to tell you he doesn't want you paddling."

Harry got to his feet. "No way, young lady. I've toughed out this shoulder of mine for months now. I'll survive. Holding on to a paddle might not be the best thing in the world for it, but I'm not going to cry uncle. Don't put me in a wheelchair."

Michon moved to where she could watch Chas, not caring whether anyone was observing her. She found that if she narrowed her eyes enough to make the world take on a hazy appearance Chas blended into the landscape. His feet were locked firmly onto the ground; his flesh had been branded by the elements. His eyes saw what others didn't. His ears caught private wilderness sounds. This was where he belonged, where he wanted to be.

Why? Why had he chosen this life and not the comforts most people took for granted? Was it born in him, or did Bear, the man who became his father, shape him? Had he ever wanted another kind of life?

Michon stepped closer, admiring the quick but sure way Chas was running his strong, tanned fingers over the canoes' hulls, looking, she guessed, for imperfections. Was he born two hundred years too late? Did he belong with fur trappers, explorers? He looked as though he could hold his own with Lewis and Clark. Hardships? He would accept them without complaint. How would he have spent his nights two hundred years ago? Would he have taken an Indian maiden as his wife? Would it take that kind of woman to understand him? Would he curl up with her under a blanket on a cold night and make her forget everything except flesh against flesh, two hearts pounding together?

Michon gasped, shaken by the intensity of her emotions. Thank heavens no one could read the naked thoughts she knew showed in her eyes. There was no denying the fact that she was looking at Chas with an Indian maiden's eyes. And, like an Indian maiden, she was pleased with what she saw. He was a man built for the wilderness. He had lean hips, powerful leg muscles,

avoiding the fact that April had been part of that last time on the John Day.

"They did. But they had to fight every other rodent for miles around." Chas released Michon's arm and looked into an opening that had once been a window. "No more grain. Now it's time for the cattle to take over."

"There are cattle in there?"

"Not now. But they take shelter here during a storm. Wouldn't you?"

Michon looked up. The window and door frames were still in place, but the light in the interior came from the spaces now exposed on the roof, as well as gaps that had developed in the walls because the wooden side boards had dried and shrunk over the years. "It's hard to believe that a family had once called this proud old wreck a home. It's coming full cycle, isn't it?" she observed softly, torn between a feeling that she was touching history and the distraction of Chas's presence. "I mean, once these timbers were trees. Before much longer they'll return to the earth."

"That's an astute observation. A proud old wreck. Are you a philosopher?"

"Not usually," Michon admitted. She ran her hand lightly over the door frame, wincing slightly because of the thousands of splinters jutting out of the dark wood. "I get that way sometimes when I'm listening to music or giving my life serious thought."

"Do you do that often? Think seriously about life?"

Michon turned so she could face Chas as she answered. "I didn't use to. But I seem to be doing a lot of that lately. There's more space to think, now that I'm away from the city, from my job. But I'm not

guage, at least about what the old building meant to them.

"I wanted to. April would never come inside."

"Don't!" Michon flattened her fingers against Chas's mouth, pressing harder than she should have. "I don't want to hear about April."

Gently Chas pulled her fingers from his lips. "I'm sorry." His hands were sandwiching Michon's fingers, warming her.

Michon looked up into his eyes, saw how dark his pupils had become, and shrank back instinctively. Whatever Chas's thoughts, they were deep, maybe deeper than she wanted to know.

"Are you afraid?" he whispered. "Of me?"

"No. Maybe it's this place," Michon stammered. "The ghosts." That was a lie. What she was afraid of was herself, her responses to him.

"I'm not interested in ghosts." Chas's voice had become husky. "Michon, do you have any idea how beautiful you are?"

She shook her head. Should she walk away? Could she? "Please don't tease. You said that before, when I looked like a drowned rat."

"No, you didn't. You looked natural. Like I like a woman to look. Not at all like the first time I met you. You were wearing all that makeup then. I couldn't tell where the real you was."

Michon ran a nervous hand through her hair. "Well, this is the real me, all right," she laughed self-consciously. "This is about as natural as I can get." Her jeans had dried on her and now clung to every inch of her form.

Chas responded by taking her in his arms, locking his

sciousness, but now was not the time to wonder where the words had come from. Later, maybe. Chas's arms had tightened around her waist, his fingers finding the soft outline of her ribs under the blouse. Her breasts found a home against his chest. She stifled a moan only by pressing her lips more firmly against Chas's, by opening her mouth slightly. Her flesh, separated from his by layers of fabric, had been sparked by something that came from both within and outside her. She felt physically weak and yet filled with a strength she didn't know herself capable of. Michon was a thousand miles from the cool employee who could discuss the benefits of a raw silk dress with a woman with the money to purchase the garment. This Michon knew or cared nothing except that she wanted—needed—to have the fabric barrier torn away.

As if he sensed her need, shared it, Chas gently pushed up the hem of Michon's blouse until his strong fingers were caressing soft flesh. This time there was no way Michon could keep her animallike moan locked within her. The civilized woman she thought she was melted away and was replaced by a primitive creature, hungry for adult sensations. She knew what it meant to be a woman. But until now she hadn't known how overriding that power could be. The first slivers of light from the moon had found their way through the openings in the ancient roof, but Michon felt no shame as Chas undid her buttons and brought his lips down to flick across the line of her collarbone.

Michon sobbed softly, pressed her body against his hard one, and surrendered completely to the emotions flaming through her no longer weary flesh. She'd been touched before, been awakened. But her response had

"I don't want to talk about it," he continued. "I just want you to understand how I feel."

How do you feel, Chas Carson? Have you forgotten April and the secrets that go with her? Are you falling in love? Can you love again?

Those weren't words Michon could expose to the night air. They were, she knew, better locked inside her. Instead she relinquished her grip around his neck and brought shaking fingers to the buttons of his shirt. Undoing them was a difficult task because she could think of nothing save touching his flesh, feeling their bodies pressed together. Her legs trembled, almost deserting her. Finally she was able to push the faded cotton away from his chest. It took courage and strength she wasn't sure she was capable of, but she brought her lips to the softly curling hairs on his chest and took them gently between her lips, toying with the hairs as a mother toys with the down on a baby's cheek. Her tongue licked across the ridge of his collarbone. Her cheeks caressed the deeply tanned chest.

This was it! This was what she'd been wanting from the moment Chas Carson first entered her life.

"Don't do that if you want me to stop," Chas groaned in a voice she barely recognized.

"I don't want you to stop. Ever."

Chas reached behind her and freed her of her bra. As it fell to join her blouse she closed her eyes to savor the fullness of her emotions. His hands—those incredibly competent hands—were cupped around her breasts, awakening in them sensations too long denied. She felt her nipples harden until they pressed against his palms. He knew. He had to know how completely he held her.

"God," Chas moaned. His hands found their way to

ence, to keep her wits about her. Her heart had never ruled her head.

But tonight, here, with Chas, she was losing control. Giving her soul to him completely.

She didn't care. It was what she wanted. Needed.

The sound that split them apart barely reached her. She would have ignored it if Chas hadn't stiffened, muttered a curse, and released her to reach for his shirt.

blow on it. The water feels so good." Shanna turned embarrassed eyes on Michon. "It was my own fault," she stammered. "I was thinking of someone—something else. I didn't even think about that skillet being hot."

Michon winced when Shanna turned her hand over to reveal her reddened palm. "At least there aren't any blisters. It doesn't look like a major burn." Michon said in a tone she hoped would reassure Shanna.

"Get my first-aid kit," Chas ordered. "There's some burn ointment in it. We'll put it on once it stops hurting."

Michon straightened and hurried over to where Chas's belongings were. She felt somewhat slighted because of the stern tone in Chas's voice, but she tried to convince herself that he was simply acting as a group leader should in an emergency. Michon located the first-aid kit and returned it to Chas. At his orders, she dug out the ointment and gauze bandage that should be applied to insulate the burn from the air. "Try taking it out of the water now," he told Shanna. His voice was soft and comforting, as if he were talking to a three-year-old instead of a careless high-school student.

Shanna lifted her hand out of the water, but after a few seconds plunged it back in again. "Not yet," she groaned. "Lord, that hurts. Stupid, stupid. You'd think I was smart enough to figure out that a skillet over a fire would be hot."

"I'll stay with her," Michon offered.

Chas stared at her as he debated her offer. Finally he nodded and straightened. "Put on plenty of ointment. It should be washed with soap first," he said as he turned to leave.

herself. "I don't know many women who can go through their lives without needing a man once in awhile." *Like me, now,* she added silently as she admitted her body's restless, aching messages.

Shanna gave her a shy grin. "Of course I don't mean it. I wouldn't be mad at Skip if I didn't like him. But there's nothing wrong in letting off a little steam, is there? Look, I really mean it about being sorry I interrupted whatever the two of you were up to. He's quite a man."

Yes, he is, Michon answered silently. "Do you want to try taking your hand out of the water again?" she asked. "It shouldn't hurt once we put that ointment on it."

A few minutes later a bandaged Shanna was wiping dirt off her knees as Michon carefully repacked the first-aid kit. The campfire had been replenished, and several attempts at roasting marshmallows were being made when Michon and Shanna joined the group. Shanna wandered off to tell her experience to several other girls, and Michon took refuge by sliding in next to Harry. She didn't even look around for Chas; she was afraid her eyes would give away too much, should anyone see her looking at him. She wrapped her arms around her knees, trembling slightly from something that had nothing to do with the cold.

"Everything under control?" Harry asked. "I'm afraid I wasn't much help. Not moving as fast as I should."

"How are you?" Michon asked, grateful for yet another excuse not to think about what had almost happened in a homesteader's house.

"As the doctors say, about as well as can be ex-

"It's good advice. We don't get hurt as much if we can react that way."

"But it isn't always easy," Michon whispered. "The heart can be pretty powerful."

"So can hurt, Michon. That's what puppy love is about. It's painful when we're in the middle of it, but we come out of it a lot wiser. Puppy love is designed to prepare us for more mature relationships. Hopefully most of us learn that falling in love isn't like it is in the love songs. There's no guaranteed happy-ever-after in real life. If we learn to settle for someone we're compatible with, who we share common interests with, who we feel good around, that's not too bad, is it?"

Michon nodded, but inside she was arguing. Compatibility? Shared interests? That was friendship, not love. Love was feeling a man's hands on her body and wanting the moment to go on forever, to build until there was no stopping the ultimate outcome. Love was a shared kiss, eyes that saw through to each other's core and stripped away the protective layers.

Love was making love in a decaying house and thinking it was the most perfect spot on earth. Michon stopped herself short. They hadn't made love! Reality had pulled them apart before it could happen.

But what if Shanna hadn't been burned? What would joining her body, her heart, her mind, with Chas's have been like?

Michon stifled a moan, drawing away physically from the feelings her thoughts had ignited. It had almost happened. And—right or wrong—Michon knew she would never regret making love to Chas. There was something rare and special about him that went far beyond the physical. He might be scarred from his experi-

"Yeah? Well, then it's time you got to know each other better, because I think there's something between you two." Harry sighed. "Let me tell you something. Let an old man impress you with his wisdom. I'd been married about six years when I met this woman. Don't be shocked. I may be a teacher, but I'm still human. My wife and I already had two children and another on the way, but when Karla came to the school I stopped thinking about my kids, my job, the house I was buying. Karla was interested in the same things I was. We were both teachers, so I guess that was natural. But my wife, well, I was the guy she called when she was running out of milk and couldn't get to the store. That's what I was to her. She was the woman I made love to between night feedings and early-morning cartoons. We had a lot of commitment to each other but that was all. I couldn't remember why I'd married her." Harry sighed. "I knew it was all dreaming on my part. It was too late for a flaming romance. I mean, I was married. I had no intention of turning my back on my family. But Karla—Karla was special. We were on the same wavelength. I should have met her years before I did," he finished softly.

Michon sat in silence for a few minutes, lost in the words Harry had spoken. Harry, the practical, aging, competent teacher was also a romantic man. He had just confessed to a hopeless, romantic love. Should she feel sorry for him? "The honeymoon can't last forever," she said finally. "If you'd married Karla she'd have become your wife. You'd be stopping off at the store for her. There's an awful lot of the everyday in that kind of situation, isn't there?"

"True," Harry acknowledged. "But I can still

completely to Chas. That they were unmarried, that he hadn't declared his feelings for her, did nothing to alter her feelings. It mattered not at all that she wasn't sure what it was she felt for him.

Chas Carson was the kind of man Michon had been looking for since she'd discovered the difference between men and women. That's as far as her thoughts went on a moonlit night by the John Day River.

Michon took a deep breath, held it, and then let it slowly escape. She was restless, trapped in her thoughts, her needs, acutely aware that only a return to the ancient house and a culmination of what had begun several hours ago would still her trembling fingers, satisfy her hunger for more oxygen. This was no case of puppy love, satisfied with holding hands in a school corridor. The schoolgirl had become a woman with a woman's needs.

Michon, he's turned you on. And no cold shower is going to take the place of his arms, his lips, his body.

Savagely she shook her head. Chas wasn't around. She'd have to deal with her emotions on her own. After another deep breath she returned to the campfire, called by the pure, solitary tones of a single guitar caressing the night. As she came within the circle of light offered by the fire she recognized Shanna's friend Skip as the young man fingering the guitar. Michon dropped to the ground where the fire's heat could reach her. Shanna might be right about Skip after all. The skinny young man might not be the best looking male in the group, but he had the skill to turn the guitar into an instrument capable of turning thoughts into dreams. He knew more than chords. He could breathe life into the night. Michon settled herself cross-legged on the

been a wrestling match. I don't want to inflict them on anyone else. How's Shanna?"

Shanna? He wanted to talk about Shanna? How could she with him so near? "She's okay." Michon took a steadying breath. "See the boy playing the guitar? That's the one she was thinking about when she picked up the skillet. She likes him." Were they really having this tame conversation? He was touching her. Was her body revealing her emotions?

"I thought as much. I didn't know who had distracted her, but I figured it had to be someone special. Where were you when I came up behind you?"

"What?" Michon tried to turn around to meet his eyes, but it would require leaving the shelter of his arms. She couldn't bring herself to do that. She wanted to remain sandwiched between his legs, feel his breath on her neck. If she didn't move maybe he'd never remove his hands from her shoulders. "I was here."

"But your thoughts weren't. What were you thinking about?" Was his voice usually this husky, or was she only imagining the change in it?

Michon kept her eyes open to reduce the risk of returning to her disturbing daydream. "I'll borrow your words," she sidestepped. "My thoughts don't make much sense either. I was just listening to the music."

"He's good," Chas said and then lapsed into a silence Michon didn't break.

They sat together for perhaps half an hour listening to the music, watching the play of firelight and night. Michon struggled to control her breathing, acutely aware of Chas's arms around her. His breathing registered along the length of her back, breathing that seemed to her deep and regular and undisturbed by the

through the openings between the old boards they didn't acknowledge it. Other thoughts consumed them. Michon had put on a lightweight jacket but offered no resistance as Chas unzipped it. He kissed her softly on the forehead before removing her blouse. Their mouths locked together as his fingers freed her of her bra. Her breasts responded to the cold night air, to the expectation of what she knew would come. Michon groaned, eyes closed against reality, savoring every moment, giving herself up completely to the sensations coursing through her body. She tried to help Chas out of his shirt but her fingers refused to obey her commands. She had to stand, trembling, as he revealed his broad shoulders, muscled chest, tapered waist, to her.

"Michon," he started.

"Don't talk," she moaned. Her shaking fingers traced the ridge of his ribs. She pressed her cheek against his chest, taking strength from the contact. "Chas, I want you. Not words."

Now Michon knew where Chas had been earlier. Stretched out on the floor was his opened sleeping bag. She acknowledged his thoughtfulness, wondering briefly how he could have been so sure that they'd return here, dismissing the thoughts because he was too close for her to think of anything except him.

Chas again unzipped her jeans; all the time his mouth claimed hers. She shivered briefly when she was entirely naked, but forgot the cold as his hands covered her breasts and filled them with the heat in his palms. Her own hands were exploring the perfect outline of his ribs, recording the feel of a strong backbone encased in tanned flesh. Her lips touched and tasted the softly curled chest hairs bleached by a lifetime spent

locking them together from lips to toes. She pressed her body eagerly against his, loving the lean, strong feel of the man. Tears welled up in Michon's eyes, drying quickly in the night air. Tonight felt so right! Did he know that her heart was as totally committed as her body?

She had no idea how much time had passed when she again became conscious of her breathing, the cold, the night sounds. She buried her naked body against Chas's, taking warmth from him, savoring his maleness. "Thank you," she whispered.

"Isn't that what I'm supposed to say?"

"I don't care. Chas?"

"Don't talk." He stopped her by placing a warm hand over her mouth. "Now it's my turn to tell you to be quiet. I want you to spend the night here. Will you sleep with me, I mean?"

"Yes." Yes! Did he really think she could return to her own sleeping bag after what had happened? In the morning they would talk. About love. And the tomorrows of their life.

I do—'' His mouth against hers stopped anything he might have said.

The lovemaking they shared that morning was, if possible, better than the night before. Last night Michon had felt unsure, a little afraid that something or someone would disturb them before the final, shared moments. Even with Chas's lips on her throat she couldn't shake off the memory of a woman who had made him a wounded member in the world of men and women.

But this morning she tossed April from her mind and surrendered to the warmth that built within her, gave herself completely and without reservation to the man who had taken over her life, her heart.

Afterward she lay unmoving as Chas dressed in the shadowy interior. Where their lovemaking might lead was something she would think about later. At present she couldn't imagine ever asking for anything more. She watched him without shame, taking note of the corded muscles in his legs, the fine hair covering his chest, the strong line of his collarbone. "You're quite a physical specimen," she observed as he pulled on his shirt. "I feel sorry for all those men who dump their money in health clubs, when they could look like you just by working outdoors."

"And you look like a lazy cat. Are you going to spend the morning there? People are going to start looking for us. And talking."

"Let them talk. I may not move all day."

"Is that so?" Chas stepped toward her, the challenge in his eyes. Before she could move to defend herself, he'd unzipped the sleeping bag and thrown back the

But she couldn't. Last night and this morning had been perfect. She wasn't going to risk shattering those memories by bringing up reality. She was falling in love. It was that simple. Could he do the same?

Chas had left by the time she was lacing up her tennis shoes. Michon took a moment to roll up the sleeping bag and run her fingers through her hair, and then stepped outside to meet the first rays of sunlight coming over the eastern Oregon mountains. She'd spent the night in Chas's bed. No wonder the morning was glorious.

Breakfast and breaking up camp was a hurried affair that morning, since Chas had estimated it would take the group close to eight hours to reach Clarno, some thirty-three miles farther along the John Day. As Chas was explaining where the group might have to stop should the winds pick up, Shanna slipped close to Michon and gave her a quick hug. "I won't tell anyone," the teenager said softly. "I saw Chas and then you coming out of that old cabin. See, I was right. You two are right for each other."

An hour ago Michon might have agreed, but Chas hadn't looked at her, much less spoken to her since leaving her side. She had no idea what to make of that, let alone guess what he was thinking. "I hoped no one would know."

"Why?" the teenager asked. "If I were a little older and Skip wasn't around I'd probably have eyes for Chas, too. If he had a beard he could pass as a mountain man. What a hunk!"

Michon had to laugh. Joking with her new, younger friend was much nicer than trying to follow Chas's moods. "I don't think Chas thinks of himself as a

Michon shook her head. She had been a little stiff when she woke up, but after moving around for an hour with the morning sun on her shoulders, she felt limber, ready for the journey. "I don't know," she hesitated. She wanted to share the day with Chas. But was she being selfish, robbing Harry of his pride? She thought of how fiercely her own grandfather had clung to his independence, how much he'd hated having to admit that he could no longer get around without a cane. Michon, more than her hardworking, preoccupied parents, had been aware of her grandfather's pride. Harry's feelings about pulling his own weight were the same. Her wanting to be with Chas wasn't as important as Harry's needs. Finally she nodded. "Chas might wonder, but all right."

"That's my girl." Harry sighed and forced a smile. "You know, for a city girl you're not doing half-bad. I thought you might be crabbing and complaining by now, but you're not."

Michon laughed. "No, I'm not, am I? I wasn't sure when I started this trip, but I've got the bit between my teeth now. I'm going to see it to the end if it kills me."

"It won't," Harry said as they walked down to the river. "You're strong and young."

"Not every woman wants to be told she's strong, you know. That's not the greatest compliment in the world."

"Well, I mean it as one."

Michon met his eyes. "Thank you. That's how I'll take it."

She was feeling much more confident than she had the morning before, as she helped load Harry's belongings into the wooden canoe she'd shared with Chas. It

pit of her stomach. It had been perfect last night. What was wrong now?

Harry interrupted her thoughts. "I'm sorry, kid. I'm not helping things between you and Chas, am I? Maybe I should have kept my big mouth shut."

Michon shook her head. It would be selfish to put her desires before Harry's obvious need. He wasn't asking that much, just a little understanding from her. "I'll talk to him tonight," Michon said lamely. "I don't know what he's upset about."

But maybe she did. Or at least she was afraid that the problem had a name. April. Chas had been able to put his lost love out of his mind last night and early this morning. But what they'd shared in a sleeping bag was only a fantasy, a momentary interlude. Did she really believe that he'd come as far emotionally as she had? She couldn't expect Chas to lay down the memory of the woman he'd carried with him for so long. Forgetting April, if he ever did, wasn't going to be accomplished in a single day.

And yet it hurt. Michon had given him her body because she was ready to declare herself to him. Her surrender, her desire to make love, came because her heart was involved. Did he realize that? Was it impossible for him to involve his heart in what was happening between them?

The answers weren't here, on the river. What the river offered was a distraction from her thoughts, the need to concentrate on practical matters. Even as they left Twickenham Bridge and drifted past Jennie's Peak, reaching into the skyline, Michon realized that she was doing a lot more of the work of paddling than she had yesterday. Harry's paddle barely skimmed the surface

woman. At least Jennie had a peak named after her. But Michon was sure Jennie would have preferred happiness in her life to immortality in the form of a mountain peak.

As Michon concentrated on keeping up with Chas's strong back in the canoe ahead of her, Harry told her about the early attempts to develop coal mines in the area. Her ears pricked up as they reached Red Rock, and Harry explained that the area was famous for its fossil beds dating back some sixty-six million years.

"I feel like I'm walking in the middle of history," she said softly. "I wish I'd paid more attention to history when I was in school."

"It's never too late to learn," Harry said over his shoulder. "Have you thought about going back to school?"

She hadn't, at least not consciously. But as she fought to keep her thoughts away from the lead canoe she gave voice to the restlessness that had brought her to the John Day. "I don't think I want to go back to my old job. In fact I'm sure I don't. I went to college after high school, but—well—I guess I was eager to make my mark on the world. I'm ready to take another look at my future. I just wish I knew which direction I should take."

"You could work part-time and go to college. A lot of people do that," Harry pointed out. "Don't mind me. I realize that not everyone is as dedicated to the educational field as I am, but I don't think we should ever stop learning. Michon, you're young. If you don't like what you're doing, change it. It's too late for regrets when you're my age."

Michon bit her lip. "You know what I'd like?" she

settled into an uneasy knot. What was she doing? If she were where she wanted to be, in Chas's canoe, the thought of the rapids would fill her with a sense of excitement. It was a different story now that she knew how much Harry depended on her.

As if he knew she needed distracting, Harry pointed out a flat area called Liberty Bottom on their right. "From what we've been able to figure out, it was named during the Centennial Year of 1876. I'm sorry, but there's no way you can get away from history around here."

There wasn't, Michon agreed, as she took advantage of the quiet water they were traveling on now. It was hard to get much of a sense of history while living in the middle of a modern city. But the John Day was alive with it, capable of bridging the gap between past and present. The more she thought about it, the more the idea Harry had brought up excited her. Had she kept any of her old history books? But better than reading about history was getting Harry—or Chas—to tell her about the river's past.

She was concentrating so intently on the barren landscape, trying to feel what the early settlers might have felt, that she almost ran into Chas's canoe before she realized that he'd stopped and turned sideways in the river. He waited, back paddling easily until the rest of the canoes were gathered around him.

He was looking at Michon as he spoke. "We'll be reaching Homestead Rapids soon," he said loud enough to be heard above the constant rumble of moving water. "Just before we get there we'll turn slightly to the left around a bluff. The river will start to pick up speed. Stay left. The river smashes into a small bluff in the right

to nights on the John Day. Days belonged to the job she'd taken on.

Michon leaned forward, placing the bulk of her weight on her legs. At the same time she rose off her seat in order to raise herself in the canoe and improve her view of the oncoming rapids. Her hands clutched the paddle. She wanted to give Harry a brave smile as he turned to glance at her, but she wasn't sure how well she pulled it off. The sound of the river grew in intensity as the sleek craft surrendered to the water's will.

As sprays of water hit her face and dampened her clothing, Michon said a silent thank you for the sense of security her life vest gave her. Even if she wound up on the bluff, at least she wouldn't drown.

But she wasn't going to let the right channel claim her! Michon fought the countercurrent with every ounce of strength in her arms and shoulders, relishing the opportunity to test herself. As she gave herself up to the essential task of following Chas's lead, she realized that, for the first time today, Harry was doing his share of the work. Cold spray hit her face, roaring water filled her ears. For a few seconds nothing existed except the river's strength and her role in it.

Because of the speed of the river through the rapids they were safely past Homestead Rapids before tension and alertness had time to fight fear in Michon's mind. She leaned back, lifted her face, and threw her damp hair back over her shoulders. She'd done it! And without Chas to lean on!

"No more?" she heard Harry groan. The look on his white face as he turned back toward her told the story. The journey through the rapids had been torture for him.

what they want it to, and nothing ever changes their minds." He turned briefly to give her a wink. "You go with the flow. You accept what's happening on the river and don't fight it."

"I guess that's true," Michon admitted. "Watching Chas yesterday helped. He's a good teacher."

"He is good, isn't he?" This time Harry's wink had a decidedly teasing quality to it.

Michon blushed and dropped her eyes. How much did Harry know?

"Don't be embarrassed," the older man continued. "There's nothing like a moon and a little guitar music to get the old romantic juices flowing, is there? I'm not so ancient that I don't know that. Do you mind if I give you a little advice?"

"Of course not," she said, not sure what her real reaction was.

"Don't try to change Chas. Don't try to put a tie on him or bring him out of the wilderness. It isn't going to work."

Michon's eyes were locked on the strong back ahead of them. "I'll never try to change him. He's perfect the way he is," she said softly. "This is where he belongs."

"I thought you might say that. There aren't many men like Chas Carson left in this world. It's a breed that should never become extinct. Most of us settle for working for some large company, making house payments, spending our winters sitting in a warm house. There aren't many who run their own businesses, build their own homes, feel more at home on a river than in a car."

But Chas does. And that's what I love about him.

Love? There was that word again. They hadn't

She squeezed her eyes tightly against the wave of thought washing over her and fought her way to the surface. "I'm ready for another history lesson," she managed. "You said something about there being a Burnt Ranch Rapids. Where did the name come from?"

Harry chuckled. "Changing the subject are you? All right. If that's what you want to do, I'll play along. Burnt Ranch? We can thank the Indians for that. The story goes that a couple of men were living in a house near here in the eighteen-sixties. One day they forded the river and were gathering driftwood when a band of Indians headed toward the house. Since their rifles were in the house, the men jumped on their horses and crossed the river, hoping to get to the house before the Indians. They didn't make it."

"They were killed?"

"Don't get ahead of me, young lady. I'm trying to make this story good. When the Indians started waving the weapons around, the two men decided they weren't much of a match for Indians with rifles, so they took off for the high country. By the time they found some packers to help them fight off the Indians, their house had been ransacked and set afire. No one sent the Indians a bill for the damage. A house was eventually built there, but the name stuck."

"Does anyone live there now?"

"No. Not much reason to live around here now. Gold was discovered here in the eighteen-sixties. That's what brought men here for a while. If you want to learn more I suggest you borrow one of the books I brought with me."

"You aren't going to give up on me, are you? You'd probably give me a pop quiz on it if I read the book,"

Chapter Eleven

The expedition was still upstream of the rapids when Chas signaled for the others to follow him as he headed for a sandy beach opposite a large bluff. Michon landed her canoe near Chas's, jumped ashore, and then held the craft steady as Harry slowly got out. She longed to say something to Chas, but it was clear that he was concentrating on the river ahead of them and not on her.

"I'm going to climb the bluff and take a look at the rapids," Chas explained when he had everyone assembled around him. He pointed at three of the boys, indicating that they were to join him. "If the river were a little higher we could cheat the rapids by staying to the right and cutting inside the curve of white water. Unfortunately there isn't enough water for that."

"Should we carry our canoes around the rapids?" one of the girls asked. "The river sounds angry."

Chas laughed, but his eyes were serious. "A river always sounds angry when it's battling its way around rocks. No. We came to conquer this river, not the other way around. I need to get a look at the rocks. Climbing the bluff is the only way to get a decent view of them. The rest of you might want to have something to eat,

Harry nodded, a motion that caused his face to contort. "Darn shoulder! Doesn't want me to move at all. That makes me the captain, doesn't it? I just hope Chas doesn't find anything that might give us trouble."

Michon couldn't agree more. While she was in the canoe, concentrating on moving the canoe smoothly down the river and taking in the landscape, she didn't have much time to think about what she would do in an emergency. But they were on shore now. The river was a few feet away, a relentless current drawing them toward Burnt Ranch Rapids.

Michon was making sure that the group hadn't left behind any garbage after their quick lunch when Chas and the boys returned. She handed them sandwiches and waited to hear what Chas had to say.

"It's moving a little faster than I'd like it to. There are some rocks we're going to have to steer clear of because they're close to the surface." He was looking at Michon as he finished. "We'll be staying right center the whole distance. Don't get sucked in close to the rocks. We'll be in trouble if that happens. The river drops about ten feet in a hundred yards, which means it's really moving."

That I don't need to hear, Michon thought, but she joined the others as they again entered the river. It wouldn't be so bad if she had a partner capable of doing his share of the work. She knew Harry would do his best, but Michon knew that there comes a time when pain takes the upper hand, and no matter how much a person wants to do something, it isn't going to happen.

That's what happened to her grandfather. He'd fought having to move in with his son's family after he became a widower, but then he broke his hip, and

Maybe she was out of line in the way she spoke, but he was out of line by insinuating that she needed to be led around by a leash. The man had already taken over more of her than she dreamed possible. Part of her struggled to remain free.

The cold water splashing on her face quickly erased her anger. There was no time now to think about what Chas was capable of doing to her senses, her heart. The river held all the power now.

Ahead of her, standing waves were piling up, creating higher peaks and deeper troughs. Michon rotated her shoulders toward the gunwale, punched out with her lower hand and leaned, using the bracing stroke more out of instinct than training. She had no time to see what Harry was doing, but from the pulling sensation around her, she knew she was doing most of the work.

The canoe topped the crest of a wave that threatened to spin it broadside. Michon quickly rotated her shoulders toward the water and reached out to catch a piece of the retreating wave. By twisting her torso around as far as possible and increasing the angle of the paddle bite, she was actually able to slow the canoe slightly and still maintain stability.

The strain in her shoulders made her cry out from the effort, but she didn't let up. As they reached the climax of the drop she decided to slow the canoe a little to minimize the slap into the final wave trough. She jammed the paddle vertically into the water, prying up and forward, literally letting the boat down. In the moment of rest that gave her, Michon threw back her head to toss her wet hair out of her eyes. Harry's back was a misty blur; she could barely make out the outline of the canoe ahead of her.

For some reason she didn't understand, Michon wasn't afraid. She was securely in the grip of the current, but as long as she kept her arms and legs tight against her body, she was in little danger. She didn't try to fight the water. Somehow she'd been thrown into the river's main current. Mercifully there were no more rocks waiting for her to be smashed against.

Michon didn't deny her helplessness. There was no way she could fight her way out of her captor's grip. But the river was a gentle master. It bore her steadily through the rapids, shaking her a little but leaving her unbruised. As the shoreline rushed past her, Michon's mind focused on Harry, not her own safety. Where was he? Had he hit any of the rocks?

Almost as quickly as it had begun, her roller-coaster ride ended. Michon sensed the lessening of the river's grip as the rapids gave way to quiet water. She lifted her head, dog-paddling as she took her bearings. Her clothes hung heavily on her, but the life vest kept her from going under. She swam toward the shore, her arms tired but still willing to accept the command of her brain.

She'd pulled herself onto the shore and was starting to sit up when she heard the shouts. Turning quickly, Michon focused on the figures in the water. They were too far away for her to see their faces, but it wasn't hard to make out the life vests belonging to Chas and Harry. Chas was carrying Harry in a lifesaving hold designed to keep the older man's head above water. Not far from them was the damaged wooden canoe and the one Chas had been using.

Michon staggered into the water, reaching for the swimmers as the river lapped at her chest. By reaching

tension, Harry coughed, choked, and started to breathe on his own.

Chas rocked back on his heels and turned toward Michon. He said nothing, but his eyes raked over her sodden form. Michon knew that he would find a thoroughly drenched, tired, but healthy young woman.

"Harry?" Chas said, turning back toward the teacher. "How are you? Are you hurt?"

"Of course he's hurt," Michon spluttered. She hated the high, tinny sound in her voice, but she felt like a coiled spring about to snap. She'd been there the day a heart attack had claimed her grandfather. She knew how close they'd come to facing death today. "Leave him alone."

"Leave him alone?" Again Chas turned on her. "You didn't see him hit that rock. I did. Why the hell—"

"Why the hell what?" Michon challenged, but Chas didn't respond.

He'd leaned forward again, his ear close to Harry's mouth as the older man whispered something. "He thinks he's broken a rib," Chas bit out. "Why the hell didn't you keep to the right? Was it too much to ask? You said you could handle things."

He was blaming her! Did Chas really think she'd do something to endanger either herself or Harry? "That's right!" she spat out. "Blame me. If I'd been sitting in your canoe like a dutiful little girl this wouldn't have happened. That's what you're saying, isn't it?"

Chas ignored her. "Don't move," he ordered Harry. "We'll get you out of these wet things. Maybe we can see if anything's broken."

But she couldn't leave. Michon slipped closer, staying out of Chas's reach, but still able to watch what was happening. Chas had unbuttoned Harry's shirt and was running gentle fingers over the older man's chest. Michon didn't need anyone to tell her the reason for the swollen welt on Harry's side. A rib, or ribs, had been broken.

Michon's legs threatened to collapse, and she was forced to lower her head to bring blood to her brain. Her body was trembling, reminding her of the strain she'd subjected it to. But giving in to exhaustion would have to wait. Finding out the extent of Harry's injuries was the overriding concern.

There was a large circle of teens around Harry by the time Chas finished his examination. "He's going to need to get to a hospital," Chas said. "We're going to have to make a litter for him."

"There's no hospital around here," someone pointed out. "There's not even a road."

Chas pointed. "There's a park north of here. It's on a hard-surfaced road. We'll carry him there and flag down a car. Then we can get to Antelope."

"What about the canoes, our gear? Someone's going to have to stay with that," Michon pointed out.

Chas turned on her, eyes still flashing their ebony lights. "I'm aware of that. Even we children have some sense of responsibility. I'll take three of the boys with me. We'll take turns carrying the litter. The rest of you are to wait here until we return. Do you understand that?"

"I don't think—" Michon started.

"Do you understand?" Chas's words left no room

Chas fashioned a litter for him, and then held his hand as he was gently lifted onto it. Chas and one of the strongest boys were ready to lift Harry off the ground before Chas talked to her again. When he did, his voice held no hint that they'd ever been lovers.

"I don't know if we'll be back before morning. It depends on what we find when we get to the park. I have to put you in charge."

"Don't worry. I can handle it."

"That's right. You aren't a child. You're grown-up."

Michon could only stare at Chas as he lifted the sides of the litter in his strong hands and headed north. Accusing him of not having grown up was simply a momentary emotion, words lashed out in the aftermath of the experience she'd just been through. It didn't mean anything. Surely he understood that.

But maybe he didn't.

softened her tones slightly—"I don't know about any-one else, but I'm about to starve."

Michon was impressed by the teenagers' inclination to follow her directions. She'd been hesitant about tak-ing over Harry's leadership role, but there was no alter-native. Now she realized that somewhere along the line she'd gained their respect. For once there was no teas-ing, no horseplay. When they had to, the teens knew how to attend to business. In less than an hour all of the canoes and their belongings had been lined up along the shore, and two of the boys were using strips of duct tape to repair dings in the canoe Chas had aban-doned.

Michon supervised dinner and the cleaning up, and then freed her charges to do any exploring they might want to, as long as they stayed out of the river and were back at camp by dark. Although her arms ached and her legs felt strangely weak, Michon was unable to sit still.

On foot Michon followed the river's path for perhaps a mile, her mind aimlessly recording the bend in the river that turned it north. She hung her camera around her neck and clambered up a rock that provided her with a view of the river from above. She took several pictures, and when the setting sun turned the landscape a rosy hue, she recorded that too.

The sun had set and the night wind had a chill to it by the time she turned back toward camp, but she didn't hurry. Last night she'd been with Chas. It was lonely, hollow, without him.

No! Michon shook her head. She wasn't going to think about Chas. Either they'd patch up what had gone wrong with them, or they wouldn't. Nothing was

"But to see your son die! I don't know how they did it."

"I don't either," Michon admitted. "I didn't give it much thought when I was taking history in school, but those were real people we were reading about. This"— she held up the book—"makes it much more real."

"I wish I'd had history introduced like this," Roger Parker said. "Maybe I wouldn't have gotten a D."

Someone started to tease the handsome athlete, pointing out that the only class he didn't have trouble with was physical education, but as Michon let the teens talk about what they liked and didn't like about school, she found her own mind drawing away from the conversation. Why hadn't her teachers made more use of personal accounts such as those in Harry's books? Of course that wasn't always possible, but she couldn't help but toy with the idea of seeing the rise and fall of the Roman Empire through the eyes of a soldier or slave, or even one of the emperors, instead of placing so much emphasis on dates and events.

That's what she'd do if she were teaching history to today's kids. She'd help her students see that history was nothing more than people living out their lives in the past. Those people might be dead, but their stories, their tragedies, and their successes, could still be brought to life. The lessons they'd learned could be used today.

Michon shook herself out of her daydream. She wasn't a history teacher. But as she returned to her book she felt a secret sense of accomplishment. History could live. It was simply a matter of how it was handled. Maybe Harry had a point. She loved what she was doing right now, which was a heck of a lot more than she could say about working at Chantilla.

thing except the touch of the man who had his arms around her.

Michon groaned, moved in restless agony, and focused on the distant stars. If only she could shut out what had happened today. If only she could let last night remain clear and unchanged in her heart. Every woman needed one night like that in her life.

Oh, Chas, she moaned to the silent stars. *Do you have any idea what you did to me? Do you know what you're capable of?*

It wasn't just that he'd touched her physically in a way she'd never been touched before. Somewhere, buried so deep she hadn't known it existed, was a nerve, an essence, something. That spot was now awake. It knew—wanted—one thing in life. That thing was love.

Michon was in love, as totally and completely as a woman was capable of. She was bound to Chas with a cord stronger than any she'd dreamed possible. It hurt. How it hurt! But Michon was alive in a way she'd never dreamed possible. And pain or ecstasy, it was worth it!

Chas? I love you. Do you know that? Will you ever tell me why the fire in your eyes burned so deeply as you lashed out at me? Can you see that I'm never going to be the same again? Do you care that I won't let our argument drive a wedge between us?

I'm sorry. Was that what she was going to have to say? She didn't know why Chas had reacted so violently. In truth, she barely remembered what she'd said. She would give anything to have his arms around her, his voice asking if she was all right. She understood that he had to give his attention to Harry. But was it impossible for him to turn to her in concern, too?

sleeping quarters Skip was waiting for her, and she wondered, despite herself, what had gone on between the two after she'd gone to bed. Michon had to admit that she was a little nervous about what they were going to do after breakfast. Obviously she couldn't give approval to continuing their expedition. But what were they going to do with the day if Chas and the boys didn't return?

The question didn't have to be answered. Bacon was still cooking when one of the girls pointed. Over the top of the hill came four figures, the lead one a form Michon would never forget. For a moment she stared at Chas, recording all over again his casual, yet self-confident walk, the way his jeans molded themselves to his lean hips. Michon stifled a shuddering breath, grateful that he was too far away to see the flush in her cheeks.

Chas was back. For the moment that was enough. "How's Harry?" she asked when the men were a few feet away.

Chas stared at her without warmth and then spoke in a voice intended to reach everyone. "Harry's in a hospital in Madras. We were lucky. A county sheriff's deputy was at the park. He took Harry with him. Harry was probably in the hospital before dark."

"You spent the night at the park?" Michon asked. "Why didn't you come back?"

"Carrying a man is work. Besides, there was no reason to hurry back."

Michon recoiled from the deeper meaning of his words. His feelings for her hadn't changed. Whatever she'd said or done to make him lash out was still the overriding force in his emotions. "He—was it hard on

"We're going to go on?" Skip asked. "I thought, without Harry—"

Chas stopped him. "The last thing Harry said was for us to finish the trip for him. If there's anyone who doesn't want to, now's the time to say so."

Michon bit her lip. If she wanted to preserve her sanity she should walk away now. But if she did she might never see Chas again, never have the chance to find out what had gone wrong. There was too much at stake to back down now. "I don't think there's anyone who wants to bail out," she said.

"Someone has to be responsible for the girls," he said. "That's what you signed on for."

"Thank you for admitting that," Michon snapped, to hide her turmoil. "Does that mean I'm going to get a gold star at the end of this?"

Chas ignored her comment. "You'll have to travel with me," he pointed out. "The canoe you were in isn't going anywhere."

"It was your favorite. Chas, I'm sorry about what happened to it."

"So am I," he said as he turned away.

Michon stared after him. For a moment she struggled with the impulse to hurl the cast-iron skillet she was drying at him. Instead she lowered it and laughed shakily. At least that reaction was easier to deal with than despair.

Michon didn't give herself time to think about how she felt about being in the same canoe with Chas. Because they were late in starting, she hurried to pack and load her belongings. She couldn't help but feel proud because she now felt competent with that chore.

They'd been in the river for almost a half hour be-course forced by the massive canyon sides surrounding them. Again Michon took out her camera, cutting down on the shutter speed to allow for the deep shadows.

"It doesn't bother you?" Chas asked.

"Being in the canyon? Why should it?" If Chas was determined to keep their conversation impersonal, she was going to play the game by his rules.

"I don't know. A lot of people don't like it. They say they feel trapped. This one's Rattlesnake Canyon."

"This looks like a country a rattlesnake would go for," she observed.

"And that doesn't bother you?" Chas sounded even more confused.

"Of course not. I'd dare say rattlesnakes have been here a lot longer than humans. What do you want me to do, squeal and carry on because I'm scared? I respect rattlers but I'm not going to turn into a quivering bowl of Jell-O."

"You don't have to do anything," Chas replied. "I just haven't met many women who hear the canyon's name without reacting negatively."

"Is that what April did? Did she shudder?"

"April said that if rattlesnakes were here she didn't want anything to do with the place."

Michon couldn't keep herself from shaking her head. April. Of course April had to enter the conversation. "Chas, all women aren't the same. I'm going to keep my distance from rattlers, but that doesn't mean I don't want this experience."

"I don't understand you." Chas's words were buffeted by the wind trapped in the canyon, but they still reached Michon.

tory lesson?'' she joked. ''I thought the only thing you cared about was who got into the Super Bowl.''

The boy laughed. ''My folks won't believe it. Neither will my history teacher. But I'm a lot more interested in history than I was before this trip. Chas and Harry talked a lot about the area yesterday.''

''Harry talked? I didn't think—I'm surprised he felt like it.''

The youth shrugged. ''Maybe he needed to keep his mind off what he was feeling. I think his shoulder was bothering him more than his ribs.''

''His shoulder?'' Michon frowned. ''The bursitis. He told you about that?''

''Yep. The old goat admitted that was what caused the accident. Said he didn't have any strength and couldn't keep his end of the canoe away from the rocks.''

For a moment Michon could only stare. Chas knew about Harry's bursitis. Why hadn't he said anything? She turned toward the river, but Chas was little more than a dot. She forced herself to continue the conversation with the boy for another couple of minutes and then excused herself. This tiptoeing around each other's feelings was going to end.

If Chas heard her coming he didn't make any indication. He was applying duct tape to a canoe when she approached, his strong hands smoothing down the edges to make a tight seal. Michon refused to let her eyes stray to his lean form. Instead she concentrated on the thick thatch of hair and steeled herself against what she was afraid she'd see in his dark eyes.

''We have to talk,'' she heard herself say.

Michon felt herself go weak. Trembling, heart beating a wild tattoo against her breasts, she waited for whatever punishment was coming. Punishment was in the form of a savage kiss that burned and ripped. She closed her eyes, swaying in his grip. The river sounds, the feel of the wind pulling at her hair, the small tired ache in her shoulders, all that became nothing as her entire being surrendered to the kiss that consumed her. Michon grabbed weakly at him as she struggled to keep from collapsing. Her head was flung back, legs slightly spread for balance, hungry for the pain and ecstasy she knew he was flinging her way.

"What are my feelings?" she whispered as her breath mingled with Chas's.

"The same as April's. No different. They're no different."

He was gone. Michon stood, still swaying, aching from the loss of that essential contact. Her feelings were the same as April's! How could he say such a thing? April couldn't have loved him. She wouldn't have wounded him the way she had if there'd been love. Michon would rather die than cause Chas pain.

But he was ripping her apart. Did that mean he felt no love for her?

Michon struggled under the massive weight of that cruel question as she went about the evening chores that, fortunately, had become routine. What kept her from helpless tears was a small knot of anger that became even more determined every time she thought about how Chas was drawing a comparison between her and some woman she'd never met. How could she be like April? April had turned her back on Chas—something Michon would never willingly do.

Scotsman named Farquer. Her parents worked for him and he felt responsible for her death. Farquer never married, but when he was in his thirties he fell in love with a fourteen-year-old girl. She turned him down."

"Can you blame her?" Michon asked. "There's no way they could have been right for each other."

"Age isn't everything."

"No," Michon admitted. "There are a thousand reasons why two people can't live together."

Michon sought relief from silence by attaching a telephoto lens to her camera and getting some interesting shots of an abandoned wooden wagon, a rusting wagon wheel propped against what had once been a fence, a juniper tree silhouetted against the sky. She could feel Chas's eyes on her, but didn't turn to see if she could read the message in them. She was tired of being compared to April, of constantly having her name brought up. Her only defense was to ignore the man in the canoe with her or at least to make him believe he was being ignored.

She felt as if she'd spent her entire life in a canoe when Chas finally pointed toward a sandy beach and indicated they should go ashore. Michon's legs failed her as she started to step onshore, and she had to grab at Chas for support. He held her tightly, almost savagely. "Are you going to say you've had enough?" he challenged. "You want to be home in a soft bed, don't you?"

"You're wrong," she hissed as she broke free. "I wouldn't trade this experience for anything. I don't know what I have to do to convince you of that."

For a moment lines appeared on Chas's forehead. "Maybe you wouldn't," he said softly. "After dinner I'll show you a cave."

"I like them. I try to remember what I felt when I was their age."

Chas had turned her around, so there was no ignoring his presence. "You aren't what I thought you were the first day we met."

"What am I?" she managed.

There was something sharp and guarded about his words. "What I mean is, I thought you were kind of empty-headed, thinking about nothing except how you looked. You're much more adult than that."

"Is that a compliment?" How could she go on speaking? Her emotions were wild, winged things flying erratically in the circle of her heart.

"It's always a compliment to be called an adult. Not all of us achieve that status."

Something about Chas's words frightened her. She couldn't see his face so didn't know what emotions were in his eyes. She wrapped her arms around his neck and pulled herself up on tiptoe until her mouth found his. She felt his arms around her waist, pulling her close, sheltering her from the dread she'd been living with.

Chas smelled of sage and river water and a clean wind. His body was as hard and strong as the canoe she'd ridden in all day. As she surrendered to her physical needs she accepted the knowledge that she'd never wanted anything as deeply as she wanted Chas Carson tonight. Her lips parted; her tongue sought to touch and taste him. When his hands found her Windbreaker and pulled it off her shoulders she could only sob deep in her throat.

She clung to him desperately, gripping him with a strength born of a need she was experiencing in an in-

But he seemed in no hurry to end their kiss. His breathing quickened and became deeper. They were pressed together, her breasts finding shelter in his chest, her body throbbing with an ache she could sense in him also. They'd had a fight. It was over. And the magic they'd reached before in a frontier cabin was going to be repeated tonight.

Finally he drew back, his eyes traveling slowly down her form. "Do I pass inspection?" she asked. "I feel like I'm some kind of toy you can't decide whether you want to play with."

"Play? Is that what you think?"

"No," Michon stammered, shaken by the sudden cold in his voice. "I—it was just a figure of speech."

"A fitting one." His hand dropped to his side. His eyes returned to her face. "Children play with toys, don't they? Is that what this is, Michon? You have some new game for the little boy to play."

"Chas? No! I don't know what you're talking about." She reached for him, but he pulled back.

"The hell you don't! I don't need to be hit over the head, Michon. You said you want to become a teacher. You can't want anything to do with a little boy who wants nothing more than a river to play on."

Michon grabbed his arm with fingers that punished as much as his words were punishing her. "You're crazy! Do you think I lured you here to play games? You're the one who invited me, remember?"

"What did you expect? I can't sit in the same canoe with you all day and not react." If he felt the nails digging into his arm his hard eyes didn't reveal it. "Maybe it's hard for you to accept, but I'm not interested. Little boys don't play adult games." Only then did he jerk his

Chapter Thirteen

Michon took two final pictures of the Cottonwood Bridge and removed the exposed roll of film from her camera. She held the roll in her hands, eyes on the straight, narrow bridge and almost barren hills rising around it. Bushes of some sort and a few straggly trees grew close to the river, but most of the landscape looked as dead as she felt inside. For the past two days Michon had been a silent, miserable partner in the bow of Chas's canoe. Ever since the incident in the cave she'd been holding onto her sanity with fingers that threatened to lose their grip. She could have told him that she had no intention of getting into the same canoe with him again, but some shred of pride, a feeling that she had something to prove, didn't allow her to place distance between herself and the river guide.

She took a deep breath, as if needing to take a final reminder of river and sage and high desert country back with her. Her shoulders sagged and she knew her eyes looked as if she'd been beaten on the inside. But it didn't matter. Chas had barely said two words to her since he'd left her half-naked in the cave. She wasn't brave enough to break the silence.

"Michon? Take some pictures of Skip and me, please?" Shanna asked, handing her an Instamatic camera, stopping her thoughts.

The hour's wait until the pickup and bus came into sight passed quickly. Michon found herself becoming part of one conversation after another. Despite the numb feeling that had taken over her mind, she was still able to respond to the teenagers. One moment she was talking about popular singers and sports cars. The next she was contributing to a conversation about makeup techniques or laughing at a heated argument about the fastest base stealers in baseball. Did the teens have any idea what they were giving her? Not only had their presence protected what little sanity she had left, but she relished the opportunity to be allowed a glimpse into their world. They would keep her young if she became a teacher.

Was that all there was? She craved the opportunity to test herself in the classroom, but it wasn't fair that that be the only thing she had left to look forward to. It could be different—so different—if only Chas would talk to her, explain.

Explain what? Even as Chas and several of the boys were loading canoes into the back of his pickup, Michon could sense that occasionally he was glancing her way. What was he thinking? Did he want to say something before he left? Did she have the strength to hear what that might be?

Maybe not, but hearing nothing was even worse. When Michon could no longer find anything to occupy herself with, she walked over to the pickup. No longer was she bothered by blisters. In fact she felt more comfortable in dirty tennis shoes and socks than she ever

thing I don't understand, maybe we should just drop things." She folded her arms, facing him. "Maybe this trip didn't turn out the way I wanted, but at least something good came out of it. I've changed, and I'm a lot happier with myself as a result. Maybe that's it," she said bitterly. "I grew up on this trip."

He shook his head. "You always were. It's I who—"

"Not now," she stopped him. "I've heard the little-boy business before. I don't want to hear it again, because it isn't true."

"What do you know about me?"

"Not much, I guess," she admitted. "But I've learned that I'm ready to change my life. Make it into what I want it to be. Chas, we can all change, take chances. I'm going to become a teacher. If I can stick out my neck that much I don't know why you can't take a chance on involvement, as you call it."

"Commitment to a person can't be equated to commitment to a career," Chas said softly.

"Maybe you're right." Michon felt defeated. "That's a decision only you can make."

Chas touched her cheek lightly. "You're right. Only I can do that. I'm sorry. I have to leave now."

As Michon stumbled back toward the bus she glanced down at her nails. Why did they have to be short? Burying them in April's flesh would—what was she thinking about? How could she blame April for the cloud that existed between herself and Chas?

The trip back to civilization reminded Michon all too much of a birthday party that had had to be canceled because her parents had to work overtime. The only difference was that when she was thirteen there'd been the promise of the party being held a few weeks later.

been in there long before she felt some of the dull exhaustion leaving her body. At least she had her dog to welcome her home. She still felt tired, muscles aching from having to sit in the hard bus seat, but her mind was starting to come back to life. And with that came the pain.

There was no longer any need to hide her tears, her heartache, from prying eyes. Michon lowered her head and let the water beat on her sodden hair. Under the shelter of hair and dissolving shampoo she gave in to the tears that threatened to split her head apart. She was aware of nothing except her private agony until the water turned cold.

She was shivering slightly as she wrapped a towel around her body and stared at her image in the mirror. The eyes that looked back at her were ghostlike.

"He really did it to me," Michon told Worthless. "When I finally fall in love I go all the way. I don't hold anything back."

It would have been safer if she had. That way there would be something of her left.

Michon slipped into a robe and wandered around her apartment, running her fingers over the dust on the coffee table, shrugging because a spider had left his handiwork on the ceiling light. What had she ever seen in the place? White walls, brown carpeting, drapes the color of every other drape in the apartment complex. The pictures she'd put on the wall, the few plants that managed to survive the poor light, they hadn't been enough to turn the place into a real home. Only an ugly, loving mutt gave it life.

Chas's log home was real. It had enough character, enough personality.

Michon picked up a china cat figurine and held it

he laughed. "My fellow teachers are determined not to let me forget that I just about drowned. They keep saying something about my not being a spring chicken."

"Are you sure you're up to being here so soon?" Michon asked as she sat down. She was no longer dressed in a sweat shirt and old jeans, but her casual blouse and slacks were as dressed up as she could handle.

Harry patted his side gingerly. "They've got me so taped up I couldn't reinjure my ribs if I fell off a cliff. Besides, I wanted to be here when the pioneers returned. I haven't heard everything yet, but from what I have, it was a success. I'm sorry you had so much responsibility dumped on you."

"It was good for me." Michon smiled. "I don't particularly like the idea of being considered the older generation, but at least they didn't rise up in rebellion."

"That's because you roll up your sleeves and get into the middle of things with the kids. They respect that."

Michon took a deep breath. "That's what I wanted to talk to you about," she started. Before she was fully aware of it, she had launched herself. She wanted Harry to be honest, to tell her the negative as well as positive aspects of teaching. "I'm not starry-eyed," she said. "I know it calls for commitment to become a teacher, especially on the high-school level. But the John Day has tuned me in to history. I never felt this way about the job I have now. In fact I get a little nauseated thinking about having to go on working there to finance my education."

Harry was watching her intently. "I'm impressed by

Chas feels has something to do with a woman he loved once. I have to find out what that is." She didn't add she was afraid that finding out what had Chas twisted in knots wouldn't change things between them. Instead Michon turned the conversation back around to teaching until she was satisfied that she had a clear idea of what would be expected of someone who spent her days in a room with teenagers, with parents, principals, and taxpayers looking over her shoulder. When the bell announcing the end of the lunch period rang she got to her feet, gave Harry an affectionate hug and left.

For several minutes she sat in her car, gripping the steering wheel. If April was in real-estate appraisal work she should be easy to locate. Michon squared her shoulders and drove to the nearest pay telephone. She expected to have to call several firms until she found where April was working, but she soon learned that April had her own business. So April wasn't some sweet young thing content to work under the sheltering blanket of a long-established firm. Even as Michon jotted down the address she was getting a mental picture of a competent businesswoman who did nothing on impulse. What had Chas seen in her? What could they have had in common—beyond the obvious, that is?

Michon had driven past the expensive east-side business complex before, but since she had little need for a business consultant or financial advisor, she hadn't been inside the open-air courtyard or walked up the wrought-iron spiral staircase. Everything from the massive hanging plants to the tile floors gave out the message that businesses in the complex were in solid financial positions.

Michon wrinkled up her nose as she thought about

with a black-and-white striped blouse underneath that ended in a trim collar around her long neck. Michon admitted that she never had had the knack to lift her hair away from her face like that, with curls that had to be held in place with a liberal application of hair spray.

April didn't stand as Michon entered the room. Instead she inclined her head in the direction of a chair. "You know Chas?" she asked in husky tones, lips barely moving.

"I'm not sure that's the right word," Michon supplied. She supposed she should start off cautiously, but there was so much to learn and so little time. "I want to be honest with you. I don't know what happened between you and Chas. I'm not sure I want to know. But it made a deep impression on him. I tried to get past that point, but it hasn't worked."

"Are you lovers?"

Michon shied, shocked by the bold question. "Why do you ask?" she countered.

For the first time April smiled slightly. As she did, her eyes showed life. "Good for you. I had no right asking." She laced her long fingers together on the immaculate desk. "After everything that's happened, I have no right feeling possessive about Chas. That ended a long time ago. What did you want to talk about?"

Michon took a deep breath. Quickly she told April how she'd met Chas and ended up on the John Day with him. "No matter what we were doing, or talking about, your name kept coming up. I'll be honest with you. I felt as if I was battling a ghost. I lost. I have to know why."

"He still cares?" Something, sadness maybe, flickered briefly in April's eyes. "There aren't many

the feeling that the conversation was having a cleansing effect on April. "I told you that we'd fallen in love. Michon, there were times when I looked at Chas and honestly believed I could give up everything for him. I had myself half-convinced that all I had to do was make more of an effort to know everything there was to know about his way of life. That's why I asked him to take me on the John Day with some of his friends." Something dark settled in April's eyes. "I'd been to his home, seen him at work. I thought I knew what I was getting into."

"I probably have no business telling you this, but Chas said some things about the trip. It wasn't your cup of tea, was it?" Michon asked as tactfully as she could.

April laughed. "That's putting it mildly. I can't tell you how much I missed my bed, a hot bath, clean clothes! I suppose I could have put up with it if I thought I'd never be asked to trek the wilderness again. But I knew that if Chas and I got married I'd be expected to be part of his world." April shuddered. "I couldn't do it. I couldn't go on pretending I was cut out for the rugged life. This is where I belong. I'm city born and raised. I don't want to change."

"Chas can't change either," Michon whispered. Her thoughts had gone back to a night in an aging cabin. "You can't bring him into this kind of life."

"I know." April's voice was as quiet as Michon's. "I wouldn't try. You can't put a wild animal in a cage and expect it to thrive. I'd never do that to Chas."

Suddenly April's shoulders squared. "I think I saw the end coming before he did. If there's one thing I am, it's practical. I loved Chas. I just couldn't live with him. There was no reason to prolong the pain. There was

Michon waited.

"I was pregnant. Chas wanted us to get married. I said it wouldn't work out. I—I think he understood that by then."

"Pregnant?" Michon barely got the word out.

"Chas offered to support the baby. He even offered to raise it himself. He probably would have done it. But"—April faltered a minute and then went on—"I had this business. A woman in my position doesn't get pregnant. I told Chas I was going to get an abortion, and if he didn't understand why, he was even more of a child than I thought he was. It was the cruelest, most stupid thing I could have said. The abortion was the biggest mistake of my life."

And then Michon had come along, in her ignorance throwing out the same words.

But Michon wasn't April. She was another woman, a woman deeply and totally in love with Chas Carson.

He couldn't be a woman hater. They wouldn't have had their night in the cabin if he had been. Yes, he was wary, scarred, unable to trust his emotions. But there was tenderness and the capacity to love again in him.

Was Michon the woman to show Chas that? She didn't have any ready answers, but she knew that her own life was only half a life without him.

Michon slept poorly that night and awoke without any sense of drive for the day. Should she go see Chas, try one more time? Was there anything to say? How would he react to April's regret? She managed to fill up the morning by cleaning her apartment and putting away her belongings. She knew she was stalling, but didn't push the point. Maybe the last thing Chas wanted was to have any contact with her. She tried to tell herself that a few words of explanation would clear up everything, but that wasn't true. If Chas's thinking hadn't changed—and there was no indication that it had—then knowing about a baby and its effect on Chas wouldn't put her in the arms of the man she loved.

"What would you do, Worthless?" she asked her constant companion. "You don't give me any peace when it's dinnertime. Do you think I should keep after Chas the same way?"

Her dog had no answers. It was the telephone that put her on the road to Shady Cove. She was trying to decide where to store the rubber-soled shoes Chas had given her when his voice speaking in response to her

said. Was there a deeper meaning to his words? How would he react to what she had to say about April? Would she have the courage to tell him, or would his manner reveal that what they'd shared on the John Day was history?

The sight of Chas's log home at the end of the dirt road brought back a thousand memories, memories that gave her the courage to face him—to face her future. At least he cared enough to call about the job opening. His pickup was parked out in front, but if Chas was working outside she couldn't see him. As she stepped out of her car she fought off the feeling of being watched and headed for the steps. It was just nerves that made her so sensitive. Chas wasn't the kind of man who would stand in the shadows watching someone.

She went up the stairs, her fingers once again caressing the smooth wood grain, her eyes appreciative of the way sunlight danced on the polished surface. No wonder she was dissatisfied with her own place. Who would chose stucco over the beauty of real wood? The house and Chas complemented each other well.

Michon heard footsteps and then the door opened. Chas, naked from the waist up, stood staring at her. "I saw you come up," was all he said.

"I caught you in the middle of something," she apologized, wondering where the strength to speak came from. "There's sawdust in your hair."

"I wasn't sure you'd come. It's good to see you, Michon."

He was happy to see her? She felt suddenly weak. Did he have any idea how much she wanted him? Her

I've learned. This puts me closer to the birds and squirrels. I was setting the supports today."

The logs stuck in the ground and reaching up to what would be floor level for the balcony explained the sweat still glistening on Chas's flesh and the traces of sawdust in his hair. The kitchen was full of timber and tools.

"I love it," she breathed. "You can see the whole mountainside from here. You could sit out here in the summer and watch the sun set."

"I guess."

"What do you mean, you guess? That's why you're doing it, isn't it?"

"Maybe. And maybe I'm just trying to keep busy. I used to enjoy my own company. That's changed."

"I miss the kids too," she acknowledged, although she had a gut feeling that that wasn't what he was talking about. "It was the best experience of my life. I'm just sorry Harry got hurt."

"Me too. At least he's going to be all right." Chas leaned against the kitchen wall, a gesture that took him away from her and gave her desperately needed breathing room. "We both overreacted when it happened."

"I—I just wish I hadn't said what I did," Michon whispered. They'd danced around the issue too long. It was time to face the argument that had driven a wedge between them.

"Look, Michon, it's over and done with. The past—"

"Is that what we are, the past?" Michon struggled against her tears before finding the courage to go on. "Chas, April hurt you. I understand how deep the wound goes, but I'm not April."

"I know that." He closed his eyes. The gesture gave

she had the courage to say what was pressing painfully against her temples. But if she didn't reveal April's last words they would continue to haunt her for the rest of her life. "April did more than tell me about the abortion." She waited until Chas was staring at her and then went on. "She—she said it was the worst mistake of her life."

Chas blinked. His hands were rubbing against the taut fabric of his jeans, but he seemed unaware of the telltale gesture. "That's not what she said the last time I saw her. She wasn't going to inconvenience her life with a baby."

Michon shook her head. She felt as if she were in a canoe poised at the brink of a stretch of rapids. Either her control of the canoe would stand the test, or she'd be dashed helplessly, fatally, against the cruel rocks. "She can't stop thinking about how a baby would have filled her life."

Chas turned his back on her, walked to the kitchen window, and stared out at the mountains. "It's too late for that."

"I know," Michon whispered in reply. With every fiber in her she ached to reach out and take him in her arms, but she was afraid. April was the one love of his life. Now he knew how she really felt about their baby.

Would he go back to her? And if he did, how could she go on living?

"How was she?" Chas asked without turning around. "Is she all right?"

He was asking that of her? Chas expected her to give him a report on his old love? But because being near him, talking to him—even about April—was easier than being alone, Michon supplied the answers.

was with you on the John Day. I heard a great deal of how you felt about April."

"Confession is good for the soul." Chas dropped his hammer and went back to rubbing the fabric stretched over his muscled thighs, as if the gesture were necessary to clear his thinking. Michon found herself unable to think of anything save what, if anything, would happen if it were her hands that were on his body.

"So April's still successful, is she?" Chas asked softly, seemingly unaware that he had an audience. "She's an ambitious woman. She usually gets what she wants."

"But not this time. She didn't get your baby, Chas. "I guess," Michon managed. "I don't know if she's happy."

"She will be."

When you return to her? Is that what you're saying? Michon's head was pounding, making it nearly impossible for her to concentrate on anything. "You—you sound sure of that," she said despite herself. Why was she prolonging the agony? She should turn and run. But Chas's eyes held her as firmly as any chains.

"I'll get in touch with her. We have a lot to talk about."

No! She couldn't take it anymore! Why had she come here, risked everything in this final, desperate attempt to gain back what she and Chas had begun? He was going back to April! That was all her shattered heart heard.

Michon turned away from Chas, escape the only thing on her mind. Because the sawhorses and wood were between her and Chas, she would be able to reach

senger girl, didn't I? I brought you word of your precious April. I'm sorry if you want more out of me, but that's all I'm capable of. Now, let me go!"

"I will not! In your present state you wouldn't get a mile without having an accident."

Michon couldn't deny the logic of his statement. Her hands trembled so violently that she would never be able to control a steering wheel. "I'll be fine if you'll just let me go."

"Why?" Chas pulled away from her slightly, his hands still gripping her securely. "The sun's glancing off your hair. Did I tell you that I like it much better when you do it yourself?"

"Stop it! Don't play games with me."

"I'm not playing games." His voice was low. "I don't play games, Michon. I think you've figured that out by now."

"Aren't you?" she managed. Her fingers ached to bury her nails in his flesh, but he wasn't giving her the opportunity. "What do you call my role in what's going on between you and April?"

"What's going on between me and April?"

He was going to make her say it. Was he capable of that much cruelty? "You said you were going to see April, that you had a lot to talk about. Go on. Tell her you love her. Just don't expect me to be part of it!" Michon's final words sounded brave, but she was aware of the undercurrent of desperation that made her voice tremble.

"I'm not going to tell April I love her."

For a moment Michon wondered if she'd been struck. She shook her head to clear her thoughts. "Why?" she asked, her voice failing her.

"I have to talk to April," Chas began softly. "The last time I saw her I said things I shouldn't. She did too. It wasn't a pretty scene."

"What's changed now? What do you have to tell her?"

"That I don't want her to spend the rest of her life blaming herself for the abortion."

Michon started. The caring tones in Chas's voice struck a chord deep inside her. "You mean that?"

"Yes. I didn't think I'd ever be able to admit that. Even now I'm not sure what I'm going to say. But I know April. At least I think I do. She's ambitious. She sets high standards for herself. But she's also sensitive and caring. That was what I fell in love with."

At those words once again Michon found herself struggling against tears, but she didn't let Chas know. "How do you feel about her now?"

"Concerned. Like a brother, almost. Michon, I can't say I understand April or why she did what she did. But she's regretting it, and it's tearing her apart. I hope I can say the right things."

"I—I'm sure you'll say the right things," Michon stumbled.

"Maybe." Chas laughed slightly. "At least I'll try." He laughed again, a more convincing sound this time. "That sounds pretty adult, doesn't it? I'll be playing psychiatrist, telling her not to let the past destroy the present, the future. That's pretty mature of me, if I do say so."

Michon responded to the laughter. She turned slowly, aching arms wrapping themselves around Chas's waist. "I never doubted you were anything but an adult," she whispered.

Instead of using words, Chas spoke with his body. His lips met hers, a gentle meeting that had the effect of spiriting Michon away from reality. No longer was she standing on the brink, with sunlight and laughter on one side and years of half-living on the other. She was nothing—nothing except putty in Chas's arms. His hands glided up her shoulders, along her neck, until he was cupping her cheeks, holding her gently. She responded to that touch by letting her arms drop nervelessly to her sides.

Before, it had taken his iron grip to keep her next to him, but now he needed only the softest touch of fingers against cheekbones to make her a willing participant in a kiss that stripped away everything except the sun, mountains, water, and an observant family of ducks.

Slowly, almost imperceptibly the Cinderella kiss gave way to the emotions of a man and a woman. As Chas's mouth probed for greater response, strength returned to her arms. Michon's fingers started on his cheeks, but soon dipped lower, as if hungry for a deeper taste of him; they found a home around his waist. Her breasts beat against the tanned flesh, separated only by cloth. He drew his fingers through her hair, thumbs massaging her temples until it was all she could do to keep her breath from revealing the emotions he was stirring.

Suddenly he changed position. His arms were completely around her, holding her so close she could scarcely breathe. Her mouth ached from the sudden loss as he stared out at a point somewhere above her head.

"I'm sorry."

"For what?" Was he regretting their kiss? No! He wouldn't be holding her like this if he were.

building? I was going to finish it and find some way of getting you up here before I heard about that summer job. I hoped you'd like it enough that you wouldn't want to leave."

"You're building that for me?" Tears sprang to her eyes, but she didn't try to wipe them away. Surely Chas understood the reason for their existence.

She didn't care! None of her heartache, her sleepless nights mattered any more. She was back in Chas's arms. Hungry, she reached up for his kiss. "I love you," she whispered as they met in an embrace that held no similarity to the Cinderella kiss of a few minutes ago.

Michon didn't care that her ragged breathing gave away what she was feeling. Chas's hands were on her, finding their way through the barrier of fabric, igniting satiny flesh to the emotions that had begun in a sleeping bag. Her own fingers found the outline of his ribs. She slipped her fingers upward until they found the tanned and smooth flesh covering muscles made strong by a lifetime spent outdoors. Her mouth was open, tongue flicking outward until it made contact. She closed her eyes, her mind, to anything except the pounding blood in her veins. A groan of pleasure began in her chest and fought its way to the surface.

"I want you," Chas groaned. "Michon, I want to marry you. Put you through college."

Marry! To spend the rest of her life with Chas, to brave more rivers, to learn what he meant by marathon races, to pack his equipment when he was needed for a mountain rescue, to bring wild flowers into the log home, and spend long evenings with him beside the stone fireplace? Marrying Chas Carson meant giving

Enter a uniquely exciting
new world with

Harlequin American Romance ™·

Harlequin American Romances are the first romances to explore today's love relationships. These compelling novels reach into the hearts and minds of women across America... probing the most intimate moments of romance, love and desire.

You'll follow romantic heroines and irresistible men as they boldly face confusing choices. Career first, love later? Love without marriage? Long-distance relationships? All the experiences that make love real are captured in the tender, loving pages of **Harlequin American Romances.**

What makes American women so different when it comes to love? Find out with **Harlequin American Romance!**

Send for your introductory FREE book now!

BARBARA DELINSKY
Fingerprints

Carly Quinn is a
woman with a past.
Born Robyn Hart, she
was forced to don a new
identity when her intensive
investigation of an arson-ring
resulted in a photographer's death
and threats against her life.

Ryan Cornell's entrance into her life
was a gradual one. The handsome
lawyer's interest was piqued, and then
captivated, by the mysterious Carly—a
woman of soaring passions and a
secret past.

FP-1